I0591260

...imagine turning a kaleidoscope that gives you a different sort of cat (and cat story) with every view...

The Inn, the Black Cat, and Two Halves of the Same Heart

Sometimes a Change in Perspective Makes All the Difference

Lafayette rumbled against Suzie's chest, then turned onto his back. He batted at her carefully arranged side ponytail, then at the huge swinging earrings that matched her necklace.

When she laughed, both Lafayette and Lloyd drew back in the same sweet, surprised way.

Which made her laugh even more.

This could turn out to be a fantastic way to spend the day, with a nice guy and a sweet kitty.

"I'm pleased to meet you too, Lafayette. How do you get him to leave those trees alone?"

Lloyd rolled his eyes. "Now that would be a trick. He's obsessed with knocking ornaments out. We'll probably spend the afternoon picking them back up again."

Survivors of the Malance

A Chance for Survival, or the End of Everything

Thora clucked her tongue to get Derwyn's attention before he ranged too far ahead and forgot what they were out here for. The gen mods to make these domestic cats larger and more suitable for hunting or protection left them markedly different from typical housecats. But they were still quite capable of being distractible, and stubborn about focusing again.

Filan raised up on her back legs, pushing her broad head into Thora's palm. Pointedly reminding Thora that while *Derwyn* ranged ahead after those silly fluttering birds, *Filan* was right by her side, doing what she was supposed to.

Watching out for threats. Keeping her eyes and nose out for game. And checking for traces of the PureHuman settlement that was supposed to be out here.

"Yes, you're a good big kitty," Thora said under her breath, rubbing Filan's head. "I expect you'd be off like a shot if a raccoon ran in front of us, but we won't worry about that right now."

Both Filan and Derwyn stood with their backs as high as Thora's knee, and they could easily reach her waist when they stretched. Her hand covered the tops of their massive heads, but not by much. Their huge, rumbling purrs were wonderful to go to sleep to.

Wicked Bone
A Greatly Misunderstood Gift

Katie groaned. "*Why* can't you wait until Ken gets home?"

Pashmina blinked her seductive, languorous blink and purred even louder.

Katie put the vicious, murderous feline on the dark red loveseat. Appropriate match for such horrifying bloodlust.

"Good kitty," Katie said under her breath. Ken said she had to praise Pashmina for her excellent hunting feats, no matter how messy or how often. "Brave kitty. Clever girl."

Pashmina rolled onto her back, but Katie had finally learned not to fall for that trap. Cat requests for a belly rub came with claws and sometimes teeth right behind.

The ways of the tiny house panther's hunts were still foreign and mysterious to Katie, and she thought they always would be.

In Service to a Superior Species
Offering Comfort in the Best Way Possible

After stopping to send up his perky greeting to each of

the relatively happy cats, Bitu stopped in front of Moxie's home away from home. Rather than raising his head and calling out his version of "Good *morning*," he sat, wrapping his tail around his feet.

He purred softly, watching the bars the whole time.

Janet walked over just as quietly, peering inside instead of reaching for the bars right away. Moxie had scooted her bright pink cushion as far away from the front as she could get it, nearly blocking the door to the litter box area. She'd piled a purple fuzzy blanket up on one edge like a tiny barricade, so only a hint of sleek, pure black showed.

After a few seconds, Moxie raised her head. One orange eye opened, then the other. She slow-blinked at Janet, lifted her slender tail in a dainty greeting, and snuggled down behind the blanket again.

The Magic Cat of the Hidden Springs Inn and Spa
Exit to the Best Holiday Gift of All

"Then let me welcome you to the Hidden Springs Inn and Spa. I'm Henry, and that overly friendly kitty at your feet is Zortea. Want me to help bring your bags in now, or are you hungry? Wait, she doesn't like…"

The words died in his throat as Zortea snuggled in the strange man's arms. The rather handsome strange man. She purred loud enough for Henry to hear over the music.

"Zortea, huh? Little Zee? I'm Steve, and you're about the sweetest magic cat I've ever met." He looked up at Henry. "Just show me where the food is, Henry, and I'll help myself. I'm about half-starved."

Henry shook his head, trying not to stare at Steve.

At Zortea. He was trying not to stare at Zortea.

A Kaleidoscope of Cat Tales

Published 2021 by Spiral Publishing, Ltd.
www.SpiralPublishing.net
St. Paul, Virginia

Book and cover design copyright © 2021 by Spiral Publishing, Ltd.

Cover art copyright © 2021 by Kudryashka | depositphotos.com

ISBN-13: 978-1-63992-011-2
Large Print ISBN-13: 978-1-63992-001-3
Hardcover ISBN-13: 978-1-63992-002-0

Library of Congress Control Number: 2021943294

Additional copyright information for previously published material at the
back of the book.

*For all of us who are perpetually covered with cat hair
and grateful for every last strand*

A KALEIDOSCOPE OF CAT TALES

FIVE STORIES OF CATS AND PEOPLE WHO LOVE THEM

KARI KILGORE

SPIRAL PUBLISHING, LTD.

CONTENTS

INTRODUCTION

I once heard a wonderful veterinarian say the right cat can make a cat person out of anyone. That was absolutely the case with me.

I'd been around cats over the years, and my husband Jason grew up with them. So we actually had several house cats I was reasonably fond of (the cats probably disagreed). In my previous life as a pet groomer back in the early 1990s, I was one of the few who had no trouble working with cats.

Believe it or not, if you approach it the right way, many of them do pretty well with a nice, warm bath from time to time. Cuts way down on hairball trouble, too.

My relationship with beings of the feline persuasion changed with one look into a pair of great big glowing green eyes.

Our little Appalachian Mountain town of St. Paul, Virginia, had quite a problem with stray cats several years back. My mother got involved with catching, neutering, and finding them homes, working with a wonderful local organization to help cover the costs of the surgery.

Along the way, she ended up with a big tuxedo boy named AJ, and a silky, long-haired black cat named Loretta.

I can't remember what the occasion was, or why Mom had the cats with her. But I do remember catching my first sight of Loretta. Even though she was tucked safely into her travel crate and very upset about being in there, I was struck by what a gorgeous creature she was.

Around the same time, we had a plague of mice in our house for some unknown reason. We live out in the woods and part of the house is underground, so that's going to happen. But there were way more than usual, and it was driving me nuts.

I decided it was time to hire help of the four-legged variety. And wouldn't you know it, Mom still had those two cats I'd already met.

AJ set about dealing with the mouse problem (still not my favorite part of living with cats), as well as making friends with both me and Jason and our sweet hound dog Gosamer.

And Loretta set about making it clear that my years of not being a cat person were officially at an end.

Not only that, she became a one-human cat and no doubt about it. To the extent that she truly seemed to vanish into thin air if I wasn't home. Then not long after I returned, she materialized right beside me, purring up a storm.

I was forever changed by that amazingly loud rumble and by her slow-blinking eyes.

Several years later, I somehow got it into my head that Loretta might want a companion cat, and maybe she and AJ just weren't a good match. He could be a bit obnoxious, and I thought it was possible Loretta might prefer another girl kitty for a friend.

Thus a half-grown, strangely put together cat I named Zortea joined our family. A sweet little tabby with short legs, a long body, a tiny head, and a twice-broken tail, she strutted right in as if she owned the place. I've never met a cat as bold and confident!

The thing to remember is Loretta and AJ were around ten years old by then. Fairly sedate and set in their ways, at least compared to the exuberant burst of kittenish energy that invaded their domain.

The constant demands to *COME PLAY WITH ME!!!* were not especially welcomed. The older cats weren't mean, but joining in Zortea's blistering rampages of kittenhood were simply not going to happen.

I started to get a sneaking suspicion Loretta was planning to cause me physical harm in my sleep if I didn't do something about that maddening little creature.

With her unspoken warning loud in my mind, Jason and I went to PetSmart for a restock of the jingly, crackly, and otherwise noisy toys Zortea adores to this day. As we walked in, I said something along the lines of "What we really need is a little boy cat around her age, who loves people and other cats. And black cats have a harder time getting adopted, so that would be perfect."

And yes, of course a cat fitting that exact description was waiting for us in their rescue kennels! He had the added bonus of an unusually long tail that he never did grow into.

We brought Lafayette home that afternoon and tucked him away in the same upstairs bathroom where Zortea spent a few days of adjustment before meeting the resident adult cats.

As far as feline welcomes, Zortea immediately taking up a position outside the door to play toe-bean footsie with the new arrival has to be one of the most heartwarming.

The two of them were instant chase-back-and-forth, wrestle-and-scrap-for-no-good-reason, and cuddle-together-and-make-the-humans-pass-out-from-the-cute best friends, just as I'd hoped. And the grown cats were nothing but grateful for the break.

All of that brings me to the stories in this collection, and I'm sure you won't be surprised to recognize the feline cast of characters. That's because I made no effort to disguise my furry little muses, especially in three of them.

These tales range across the genres, as my writing so often does, and each one has at least one cat as an important part of the story. So as you read, perhaps you might imagine turning a kaleidoscope that gives you a different sort of cat and cat story with every view.

The first of those is Lafayette, taking his turn in my magical inn set close to home here in the Appalachian Mountains of Virginia. *The Inn, the Black Cat, and Two Halves of the Same Heart* features a long-tailed, shaky voiced cat bringing two lonely people together for the holidays. The Hidden Springs Inn tends to have that effect on cats, and humans.

In *Survivors of the Malance*, two very different cats venture through a post-apocalyptic landscape. Even genetically modified, they exhibit many of the traits of their housecat ancestors. Don't worry though. Even with an undercurrent of darkness, a ray of hope shines through.

Wicked Bone was actually the first cat-forward story I wrote, and to the surprise of no one who knows me, Loretta was a big part of the inspiration. The other spark was my mother talking about how some people have a wicked bone. Put those two together and my imagination was off and running in rather creepy directions.

We return to the real world for *In Service to the Superior Species*, and to a real-world challenge that's still all too vivid. This story visits the beginning of the pandemic, and a woman who finds a perfect place to shelter surrounded by cats. I hope this story highlights the way so many people continue to work together to help each other during such a frightening time.

Last, but definitely not least, we return to the romantic, magical setting of the first story in this collection for *The Magic Cat of the Hidden Springs Inn and Spa*. Zortea steps in front and center, where she has no doubt she should be. This was the first time I visited the inn during the December holidays, and right away it became one of my favorite fictional settings.

In case you're worried that I've left our burly tuxedo boy AJ out, he'll be making his literary debut later this year, when the Hidden Springs Inn and Spa is all dressed up to ring in the New Year.

I hope you enjoy reading these stories as much as I enjoyed writing them.

If you're craving more romance, Happily Ever After is definitely in the air over at www.KariKilgore.com/Romance.

You can investigate all kinds of mysterious tales at www.KariKilgore.com/Mystery.

You'll find plenty of stories in almost every genre set in and around my native Appalachian Mountains by paying a visit to www.KariKilgore.com/TalesFromAppalachia.

You can also visit www.KariKilgore.com to learn more about me and find other short stories, along with novellas, novels, and more collections.

Head on over to the Confidential Adventure Club to keep up with what I'm doing next, get free stories, read exclusive content not available anywhere else, and see adorable pet photos. Hope to see you there!

www.ConfidentialAdventureClub.com

And most importantly, thank you for your support of me and my writing. It means the world to me and keeps me coming back to tell the next tale.

KARI KILGORE

AUTHOR OF ODDS AND ENDINGS AND INTENTIONS

The Inn, the Black Cat, and Two Halves of the Same Heart

For Lafayette

Our delightfully sweet black cat
with entirely too much tail

CHAPTER 1

Lloyd Fletcher sat, chin in hand, glaring at the most awful holiday stationery ever devised by a human and delivered by the print shop across town.

Twisting green holly wrapped up with red ribbon all along the top and the left side. A Christmas tree with little dots of silver foil tinsel in the upper left-hand corner, a pile of presents underneath. A black cat with big golden eyes and a much-too-long tail sitting by the presents. An annoyingly jolly Santa beside the cat, hands beside his plump red cheeks so he could shout out the headlines spelled out in swoopy gold leaf.

Merry Christmas and Happy 1988!
From Everyone at the Hidden Springs Inn!

Gag.

It wasn't so much the design, really. Lloyd thought the tree and the presents and even the shouting Santa-man were cute. Kinda merry, if he were capable of merry this year. The cat was perfect, of course. And the thought of 1988 filled him with a gut-whirling storm of excitement, fear, and anticipation. He'd be hitting the world as a freshly minted college graduate in the spring.

No, what had Lloyd about a thousand miles away from any trace of holiday cheer was that whole bit about the Hidden Springs Inn. Where he sat right now in Hidden Springs, Virginia, sulking at the registration desk.

In what had been, up until a few months ago (and still should be, dammit), the sitting room at his grandparents' beloved old sprawling house.

What they were calling the registration desk was actually Lloyd's great-great-somebody's old sideboard, turned around so all the drawers and shelves were facing away from the front door. One of his uncles had refinished the back, replacing the boring unpainted pine with polished oak. A bunch of hand-carved decorative acorns and leaves and vines made by both of his grandparents decorated the edges, with several long-faced Santas and snowflakes and even reindeer made before Lloyd's father was born.

All the napkins and placemats and silverware were stored back in the kitchen and dining room now. Instead the backwards sideboard was stuffed full of pens and paper, hard candy, and flavored toothpicks. Silly hand-drawn maps of their little Appalachian Mountain tourist town of Hidden Springs tucked way down into the corner between West Virginia, Kentucky, and Tennessee, with ads from local businesses all around the edges.

The wide, shallow drawer that used to hold forks, spoons, and knives now held a bunch of shiny new keys. Each with a little wooden number attached, also made by Lloyd's grandparents.

An exact duplicate of every key's number hung on a door somewhere in the big old two-and-a-half story house.

One for every family bedroom that now hosted passing

strangers instead of being crowded with the extended Fletcher family coming home for Christmas.

Lloyd sighed, then breathed in air that at least smelled the way it was supposed to. His granny still had a big copper pot full of spiced apple cider hot and ready for guests. It was just out here in the "lobby" on a hotplate instead of in the cozy family kitchen where it belonged.

She'd added a pot of coffee, too, and an electric teakettle with little hot chocolate packets tucked beside it.

The whole family had contributed to the festive mess all over the sideboard/desk, crowding the paper registration book so there wasn't room to spin it around for the guest's signature. Plates of every kind of cookie, cupcakes, and even brandy-scented homemade fruitcake waited for the Hidden Springs open house later that Thursday afternoon.

If the guests registered to check in on this fine Christmas Eve got here before all the party stuff and nonsense got cleared away, Lloyd would have to drag out the credit card kerchunker machine from a shelf in the sideboard and run it flat on the hardwood floor. Or maybe on one of the ugly poinsettia-covered rugs his aunt had brought in special for the first Christmas at the inn.

He hadn't expected the rectangle of shiny elf-patterned wrapping paper that covered the wall across from him, decked out with ribbons and bows around a printed sign reading "Hot Springs Spa Coming Soon!" where a bookshelf used to be.

Even the tree part wasn't right as far as Lloyd was concerned.

He'd grown up helping his cousins decorate a kinda stinky fake tree, with bendy limbs and a musty basement smell that never quite went away. The tree was still there, over in the corner of the sitting room that had been merci-lessly rearranged to become the lobby. Loaded with the same gobs of tinsel and lights and dozens of glass and plastic ornaments. All the manufactured modern stuff mixed in with goofy hand-painted or glued toothpick efforts of kids, along with more of his grandparents' expertly carved trees, elves, half and whole hearts, and sleighs.

But he knew the gaily wrapped boxes underneath were empty.

That and his family had dragged out another old tree, a silvery aluminum antique that his parents swore had been cool way back in the Fifties and Sixties. It was also loaded up with ornaments and surrounded by empty boxes, but it smelled a lot more like stale pot than the musty basement.

Neither did a thing to help his sincere lack of holiday cheer.

When Lloyd had agreed over the phone to come in and help with what might be a big, overly cheerful crowd, as all of Hidden Springs toured and caroled through businesses gussied up for the occasion, he hadn't realized how hard this whole thing would hit him.

How much it would bother him to sit here in his family holiday home, so rearranged since the last time he'd been inside. Wearing his mother's strong suggestion of dressy pants and a blue button-up shirt with a god-awful candy cane-striped tie, when he wanted to be lounging around in sweatpants and a t-shirt, reading a book or watching something silly on TV with a good-natured sprawl of cousins.

Not sitting here alone. Even the inn's sweet black cat, Lafayette, who'd run in to greet him earlier, was nowhere to be seen.

At least that meant less work picking up various ornaments off the floor, since Lafayette had already demonstrated great skill at that favorite feline holiday pastime.

Yeah, his grandparents would be here soon. Some kid his age they'd hired to help out was already a few minutes late.

That, plus roving crowds of off-key singing merrymakers, just wouldn't be the same.

He knew he wasn't a kid anymore (even if he suspected he might be acting like one). He didn't really want to be, when he was honest instead of mopey.

But Lloyd wasn't ready to give up having someplace he could come home to for Christmas.

CHAPTER 2

Suzie Bivens walked down the hallway of the new Hidden Springs Inn, doing her best to keep quiet though she had no idea why. She could clatter down the dim hardwood passage in those wood-soled sandals she used to love so much, and it wouldn't change the fact that she was late.

Late for her first day on the job she really needed, even if it wouldn't officially start until after New Year's.

Her red Converse sneakers hardly made a sound, yet another reason Suzie was sure they'd been a better choice than the uncomfortable heels she'd never gotten used to. She wouldn't be working on the inn's accounting or budget or taxes, not today. She'd be greeting people, helping keep the lobby clean, and generally making life easier for the owners.

The Fletchers, the sweet old couple who'd hired her, weren't going to be impressed with her skulking in almost fifteen minutes late.

The trusty blue Chevette her parents wanted her to trade in hadn't been the problem this time, not really. A car couldn't help getting a flat tire, and she couldn't afford another one right now, anyway. Suzie smiled when she realized that was yet another reason to be glad she'd worn sneakers. Changing a tire in heels wasn't her idea of fun.

She paused at the end of the hall. She was sure the Fletchers had said someone else would be here, but the bright, newly decorated lobby seemed empty. The prettiest pair of Christmas trees she'd ever seen stood by a huge front window. Two strips full of big silvery bells—one leather, one green fabric—hung on the inside of the oak and glass front door.

Thank goodness Mrs. Fletcher had asked Suzie to come in through the back. All those bells would make a terrible racket.

Something smelled amazing, like apples and fresh-baked cookies.

Suzie stepped out of the hallway and let out a mortified yip.

A guy had been lurking there the whole time, slumped behind the front desk!

At least he'd yelped pretty good himself.

"I'm sorry," he said, bright red from the top of his fine brown hair down to his adorable candy cane tie. "I didn't know anyone was back there."

Suzie clutched at her throat, getting a handful of the huge green beads of her necklace. She felt and even heard her heart pounding in her chest.

"I didn't know anyone was up here. Mrs. Fletcher told me to come in the back, or you would have heard those jingle bells."

His eyebrows drew down, and Suzie noticed how huge and pretty his blue eyes were.

"Jingle…"

She waved one hand toward the front door. His confused look deepened into a scowl.

"Oh yeah," he said. "Those. Supposed to be cheery, I guess. I'm Lloyd Fletcher. Can I help you with something?"

Suzie walked over with her right hand out.

"I'm here to help you, but I'm terribly late. Suzie Bivens. I'm sorry I didn't call. By the time I thought about it, I figured it would be faster to just change the tire than to run back inside to the phone. You must be related to the owners? They hired me to take care of the bookkeeping in the new year. I'm just supposed to help out with the open house today."

Suzie took a deep breath, realizing she'd blurted out way more nervous chatter than she'd meant to.

Lloyd blinked, then shook her hand with a warm, strong grip. He didn't look much taller than her five-foot-two, and his roundish face looked like it could be pleasant. Friendly.

Handsome, even.

If he ever actually smiled.

"Oh! I didn't realize you'd be... Well, don't worry about being late. Flat tires, yeah. That sucks. No one's here yet anyway. I think we're just supposed to endure the carolers and make sure everyone has something to eat and drink."

Suzie finally spotted a polished copper pot by the wall. That had to be apple-something steaming away inside from that amazing smell. The source of the cookie aroma covered the desk in front of Lloyd in just about every variety she could imagine.

She jumped and almost yipped again at a pounding noise behind her. When she turned, she realized pounding might have been a bit of an overstatement.

An absolutely beautiful cat stood at the bottom of a staircase, peering up at her with glowing golden eyes. It had a gleaming, sleek black coat, huge ears, and a slender, long-legged body. And by far the longest tail Suzie had ever seen on a cat, the tip waving back and forth a good foot and a little bit more above its back.

"There you are, Lafayette," Lloyd said. "I was wondering if you were ever going to show up."

Turned out Lloyd did have a lovely smile, one Suzie couldn't help returning. Maybe the best smile she'd seen during the whole long, dreary year.

The sound of his voice had changed, too, from a little annoyed to warm and welcoming.

Lloyd had a wonderful voice.

Lafayette raised his nose and gave out a long, wavering meow.

"Well hi there, Lafayette," Suzie said, kneeling. "Is he friendly?"

"Oh yeah. I was going to look for him before the open house. He loves to meet new people. You can pick him up if you want."

Suzie let Lafayette sniff her until he rubbed his pointy chin and the side of his mouth against her fingertips. She stroked his head, getting another of those up and down meows.

"He's so soft," she said, scooping the cat into her arms and standing. "Like a rabbit or something."

She jumped yet again when she realized Lloyd was standing right behind her. He'd moved as quietly as…well, as a cat. He was only a few inches taller than her. A pleasant change from having to crane her neck to look up at everyone. He ran his hand along Lafayette's side and got a warbling response.

"My papaw found him hanging around out front a couple of months ago," Lloyd said. "Threw a fit when they tried to take him somewhere else, so he stayed here. He'll let you carry him around like that all day long."

Lafayette rumbled against Suzie's chest, then turned onto

his back. He batted at her carefully arranged side ponytail, then at the huge swinging earrings that matched her necklace.

When she laughed, both Lafayette and Lloyd drew back in the same sweet, surprised way.

Which made her laugh even more.

This could turn out to be a fantastic way to spend the day, with a nice guy and a sweet kitty.

"I'm pleased to meet you too, Lafayette. How do you get him to leave those trees alone?"

Lloyd rolled his eyes. "Now that would be a trick. He's obsessed with knocking ornaments out. We'll probably spend the afternoon picking them back up again."

"Well, he's beautiful. The trees are too, and the whole place. And they're building a spa to top it all off, wow. Anyone would be lucky to get to stay here."

Just as fast as it had appeared, Lloyd's smile and all traces of friendliness and warmth vanished. He shrugged and shook his head at the same time. He turned and walked back to his perch behind the desk.

"They'd be lucky all right, spa and all. I hear the place has been packed full since they opened in September. Guess that's why my grandparents hired you. Good for them."

Lafayette warbled again, staring into Suzie's eyes and patting her chin with his front feet. Almost as if he were trying to apologize for Lloyd's mood swings. And his rudeness.

This fun little Christmas Eve job to help out and earn a little bit of money after a rough year might not be so great after all. Suzie was afraid it would turn into a long, unpleasant afternoon stuck with an absolute Scrooge if someone else didn't show up soon.

CHAPTER 3

By the time his papaw arrived, Lloyd's cheeks ached from trying to smile, and his jaws from clenching his teeth. People had started arriving before they were supposed to, of course.

Leaving him and chirpy Ms. Suzie Bivens with her red top and green skirt and big smile to greet them all.

Not too many people, thank goodness, but enough of a steady stream that he constantly had to pretend to be happy, to welcome them to the inn. Invite them to have cider or coffee from one of his granny's red and green cups, then a seat on the comfortable sofas arranged along the walls instead of back in the den where they'd been his whole life.

Tell them no, he didn't know anything about the spa hidden behind the wrapping paper, or when it would open. He managed not to share that no one in his family mentioned it to him at all.

To make his grumpy mood even better, Lafayette seemed determined to ignore Lloyd altogether. He spent all of his time following Suzie around when he wasn't aiming his shaky meow at some grinning stranger.

Otherwise, all Lloyd saw of the ungrateful cat was the tip

of his overly long tail disappearing around the corner, or peeking out from behind the fake presents or up in one of the trees. Suzie seemed to think it was cute when Lafayette batted the ornaments off.

Even when he grabbed the same hand-carved ones over and over again and tried to run off with them in his teeth, she thought it was adorable. She just laughed and smiled, re-hung the ornament, and carried Lafayette for a while.

Suzie seemed to think everything was cute.

She picked out Elvis's Christmas Album from the stack beside the turntable in the corner, and proceeded to sing along to "Here Comes Santa Claus (Right Down Santa Claus Lane)" and "Santa Bring My Baby Back (To Me)." Lloyd had loved that album himself when he was a kid.

His grandparents always played it when it was time to decorate the tree.

Today he stubbornly refused to enjoy one song. Not even "Blue Christmas."

Suzie complimented everyone's holiday outfits, and oooohed and aaaaaaahed over the spiced cider and the cookies. She chatted excitedly about getting to work at the inn.

She somehow managed to brighten up the whole room just by being in it.

Lloyd tried his best to ignore her, to pretend he didn't want to watch her every minute.

No one seemed to notice his Grinch-like attitude until his papaw walked in with a jingle of bells, a huge smile, and an armful of wrapped presents half the size of paperback books.

"Hey, we've got a great crowd already! I'll have to go get more fudge for sure."

Fudge?

Lloyd bit the inside of his cheek, determined to push his taste buds and their demands to the back of his mind. His grandparents made fantastic fudge all year round. Chocolate and peanut butter and maple and even coconut.

But they only made their special penuche for the holidays. Crisp and light brown, made with brown sugar and tasting of caramel and Christmas and love.

Everything Lloyd had managed to grouch and grumble and convince himself he'd never have again.

"Hi Papaw," he said, trying to keep his voice neutral. "Yeah, a lot of people have been here already."

His papaw frowned at him, and Lloyd knew he was in for A Questioning. Bad moods were allowed in this house and in his grandparents' presence, but only if you explained what it was all about.

A group of people had the bad timing to pick that moment to head back out to the next business, giving them privacy.

But before the interrogation could begin, Suzie came bouncing in with Lafayette in her arms, wooden ornament shaped like half a heart gripped in his teeth. She smiled, and both she and the cat pointedly ignored Lloyd as they had for hours.

"Hi Mr. Fletcher! Everything's going great so far. Everyone loves your decorations as much as I do." She paused for a breath. "Almost everyone."

Papaw nodded slowly as he focused on Lloyd.

"Glad to see you again, Suzie. We knew we couldn't please everyone right away. Listen, can you stack these up in front of the tree?" He traded the boxes for Lafayette, and gently extracted the half heart and bumped his chin against the cat's. "And bring in the bags in the back seat of the car? Mrs. Fletcher will be here in a little while to get them sorted out."

Lloyd only realized he'd been watching Suzie the whole time when his papaw smiled at him.

"We haven't really been fair to you, Lloyd." Papaw got himself a red cup full of spiced cider and handed one to Lloyd before settling onto the sofa. "You were away at college when we did all this. I could see from your face when I walked in that you're not exactly thrilled."

Years of experience with these loving but firm discussions let Lloyd know it was useless to argue or pretend. And with the soft tone in his papaw's voice bringing tears to his eyes, he really didn't want to.

"I wasn't ready, no. I didn't think it would be a big deal until I walked in. Then, well, I didn't even recognize the house anymore. Except for some of the decorations."

Papaw nodded and held up the half heart he'd extracted from Lafayette's teeth. The smooth, age-dark wood was about as big across as his palm, wide at the top with the side swooping down to a point. The middle had straight edges with curves in the middle like a puzzle piece.

Lloyd walked around the desk and took it, running his thumb along the middle. He'd never paid much attention to these hearts, but he'd seen his cousins playing with them.

"I'm guessing these are the ones Lafayette likes best?" his papaw said. "These have quite the history that I'd bet you don't know about yet."

As if drawn by the sound of his name, the sleek black cat darted into the room and jumped right back into the green tree this time instead of the silver one. Only his too-long tail was visible, the tip weaving back and forth to music only cats could hear.

"Yeah, that's what he's been carrying around all day," Lloyd said. "He knocks the round ones off, but he wants to keep these."

He held onto his half heart and reached in after the cat. Sure enough, Lafayette had what looked like the other half in his teeth. When Lloyd tried to grab hold of it, Lafayette twisted and turned until he managed to leap onto the poinsettia rug and streak back toward the kitchen.

"You sure he wants to keep them?" his papaw said, a laugh in his voice. "I notice he didn't go after the one you have right there in your hand."

CHAPTER 4

Suzie stopped halfway back down the hall toward the lobby, bracing herself as Lafayette ran toward her and launched himself into the air from several feet away. She barely had to stoop to catch him against her chest.

"What in the world?" she whispered. "What have you got now, you sweet goofy cat?"

She plucked one of the half hearts from his mouth, likely one she'd retrieved before from the faint tooth marks in the silky smooth wood. He pushed his head against her armpit and started purring up a storm, whipping his extraordinary tail around her ribs and back.

Shaking her head, she walked back into the living room and froze. Lloyd stood in front of the two Christmas trees, holding another of the half hearts and staring wide-eyed at her. His grandfather, Mr. Fletcher, sat on the couch, grinning fit to split, as her own grandparents might have said.

"Come on in, Suzie," Mr. Fletcher said. "Grab something to drink and sit down for a minute. Lloyd, you bring a chair over and join us. Everyone in town who hasn't stopped by already is about to come wandering in, and you both look like you've been on your feet all day."

He held out his arms for the cat, and she couldn't think of anything to do but hand him over and grab a cup. As she filled it full of the amazing apple cider that she'd already refilled from the kitchen twice, Lafayette stared at her with his big golden eyes.

He blinked soft and slow, then looked at Lloyd arranging himself in the chair.

Another blink, and right back at Suzie.

She looked at Lloyd then, and almost tripped on her way to the sofa beside Mr. Fletcher.

Instead of either the sort of grim, enforced smile he'd had when people where there or the sullen almost-scowl, Lloyd's face was relaxed. Open. More curious than annoyed for a change.

He stared into her eyes for a few seconds, then his features broke into the same warm, affectionate smile she'd seen what seemed like days ago when Lafayette came thundering down the stairs.

That smile knocked a good, solid crack into the wall of annoyance built up in Suzie's middle by his earlier behavior. That smile looked like it fit onto Lloyd's face a whole heck of a lot better than the grouchy expressions had.

"Now that Lafayette here has had his say," Mr. Fletcher said, stroking the cat's exposed belly, "let me tell you a little story or two. Those ornaments you have there and all the other wooden ones that have a bit of age on them are just over fifty years old. The Great Depression didn't bite here in the mountains as hard as it did in other parts of the country. But it did bite hard enough that we didn't have a whole lot to spare."

He leaned forward and lifted one of the whole heart carvings away from the registration desk.

"Your granny married me near the beginning of the whole thing, in March of 1931. We could bring a tree down out of the woods for our first Christmas together, but decorations other than pinecones and popcorn on a thread were hard to come by. She found some scraps of good soft wood laying around the woodpile early that winter; turned out it was basswood. So we decided we'd learn to carve our own decorations. As the years went on it was just like anything you love to do so much that you practice every chance you get. We got better. By the time we were making those puzzle piece hearts you have there, things were starting to get better out in the world. But we kept on making our ornaments."

As he paused in petting Lafayette long enough to take a drink of his cider, Suzie couldn't help but notice Lloyd kept sneaking looks at her. Quick little darting glances that weren't nearly as subtle as he probably thought they were.

And while it wasn't quite as broad as before, Lloyd was still smiling.

"I got good work in the construction boom after the Depression," Mr. Fletcher went on. "And Mrs. Fletcher cooked and helped out at a restaurant in town. Between us we could afford this big rambling house for our growing family. We hadn't been here hardly a month when the first cat showed up. Lorelei, we named her. Prettiest little calico cat you ever saw. That cat took care of all our babies and bigger kids for close to twenty years. She always made sure they were safe, and if they weren't, she made sure we knew about it."

Lloyd shook his head, but before he could say anything Mr. Fletcher nodded.

"I know, you're wanting to ask how a cat let us know children were safe. I might tell you that someday when the time is right. What I'm wanting to tell you now is what Lorelei did when our oldest kids were starting to court. We'd put up our Christmas tree with all those half heart ornaments like we always did."

He looked at Lloyd, and then Suzie, a lot like Lafayette had but without the slow blink.

"But if Lorelei liked the boy or girl one of ours brought home, she'd grab the matched set and give them out. If she didn't like whoever was visiting, she'd stay out of the tree the whole time. I never did know that sweet cat to be wrong."

This time when Suzie's gaze met Lloyd's, warm drifts of goose bumps rose up along her arms.

She didn't have to compare to know they held the two halves of a matched heart.

CHAPTER 5

A WARM FLUSH climbed from Lloyd's belly to his chest and all the way up to the top of his head. Now that he was looking at Suzie, really looking, he realized she truly did brighten up the room when she was in it.

Because she brightened up something inside of him, too.

"Now I know times have changed," his papaw said. "Young people want to have their say in things and figure it all out for themselves. I think that's a good change. That's why we decided not to tell any of you grandkids about the cats and the hearts ahead of time, and our kids agreed to do the same. All I know is this pretty little boy here decided he just had to move into this house for some reason, even when we were moving out."

He scratched Lafayette's rumbling chest, then looked at Lloyd.

"I'm sorry this whole inn project was such a surprise to you, Lloyd. We were just rattling around in here by ourselves, and the house felt so sad and lonely. All our kids have smaller families and houses of their own. We wanted to find a way for it to be full and happy again after it took such good care of us for so long."

He waved one hand toward the rectangle of wrapping paper on the wall announcing the spa would be there soon.

"When the town dug down to do some work on the plumbing and found a hot spring no one ever suspected, we knew it was the right thing to do. I sure do hope you'll forgive us and maybe even start to like it here someday."

Before Lloyd could say a word, Lafayette twisted around in his papaw's lap, then bounded over and leaped into his own. Big golden eyes slow blinked up at him again, and slow blinked over at Suzie.

I hear you, sweet kitty. Loud and clear.

"There's nothing to forgive, Papaw. It's your house, and it really does look nice now that I've quit pouting. Everybody who's stopped by so far has loved it."

He looked at Suzie, and the wide smile he couldn't seem to stop anymore jumped back onto his face.

"I'm really sorry, Suzie. I've been awful to you all day. You've been great talking to people and all. And I'm really glad you're going to help with the bookkeeping. Numbers are definitely not my strongest subject."

He stopped, not quite sure what he was saying. Did he actually want to do more at the inn when he was finished with college? There certainly were worse uses for a brand-new degree in marketing.

Lafayette stretched in his lap and let out a long, warbling meow.

"Thank you for the apology," Suzie said. "And thank you for the stories, Mr. Fletcher. I get the feeling I'm really going to love it here."

His papaw hung the whole heart back on the desk and smacked his own thighs. His face lit up brighter than the silvery Christmas tree as he got to his feet and started toward the hallway.

"I hear your granny's car pulling up outside. About time for the big party to start. You two keep those ornaments if you want. We made bunches of them. I'll head out back now, so don't worry about helping for a little while yet."

Lloyd and Suzie both blinked at his abrupt departure, then they both laughed.

"That was quite a story, huh?" Lloyd said.

"A big fish tale, my mamaw would call it. Lots of those old tales have more than a little truth to them."

Lafayette stood, stretched his long back in a high arch, his amazing tail touching the top of his head. He climbed down onto the cheery poinsettia rug and trotted after Lloyd's papaw.

Suzie and Lloyd stood at the same time, holding up their half hearts.

They were a perfect match.

"What do you think?" Lloyd said in a soft voice. "I don't have to be back at school until the second week in January."

Suzie smiled, wrapping her fingers around her half of the heart and holding it close against her chest.

"How about we spend some time together and figure it out?"

KARI KILGORE

AUTHOR OF STORMS OF FUTURE PAST AND WICKED BONE

Survivors of the Malance

For everyone brave enough to reach out
even when it might cost them everything

SURVIVORS OF THE MALANCE

THORA REMEMBERED when walking in the woods felt safe. At the height of human population—right before the crash —she'd usually felt safer, calmer, in the woods than anywhere else.

Today she could almost imagine feeling that way again.

The oak trees soaring overhead were the latest in changing for autumn, but they were already showing orange, red, and yellow. Lower down in the canopy, maples and poplars put on their own fiery show as October wound down.

Or at least she thought it was still October.

The breeze carried a refreshing chill and the earthy scent of last year's leaves turning into next year's rich soil. A few birds chattered and called back and forth, getting a wide-eyed and whisker-forward response from Thora's two patrol cats.

Solid-black Derwyn was always the first to notice anything flying overhead, so of course he never missed even the slightest sight or sound of birds.

Gray and black tabby-marked Filan preferred her prey

running along the ground whenever she could get it. She noticed the birds, flipped her tail, and resumed her scouting duties.

The river ran somewhere off to her left, evident only by the mossy growth on that side of the huge tree trunks. Memories of fish caught in that river when she was a little girl surged up in her mind. Caught, breaded with a spicy mix, cooked over a campfire, and served up hot with buttery baked potatoes and garlicky greens.

A grumble closer to a groan from the direction of her perpetually empty stomach forced her to think of something else instead.

The trail—not that Thora would call it that given any choice—was little more than a lack of undergrowth among the trees. The brown dirt under her feet was clear of any huge roots, and she was certain she felt gravel down there every few steps.

Sure, it had been unmaintained on purpose for decades now. But the traces still remained for those who knew how to look for them. And those who were brave enough.

Or desperate enough.

Thora's worn and thoroughly patched dirt-brown pants and shirt would have helped her blend in and hide back in the days when she'd wanted that. Days that stretched out years behind her, hiding out from Department of Genome Security raiders back when they still bothered patrolling. Then with the demise of GenSec, avoiding rogue PureHumans who could be just as murderous, right up until the last couple of weeks.

She'd kept her genetically modified purple hair shaved off until it finally turned gray and she didn't have to worry about hiding it anymore.

She clucked her tongue to get Derwyn's attention before he ranged too far ahead and forgot what they were out here for. The gen mods to make these domestic cats larger and more suitable for hunting or protection left them markedly different from typical housecats. But they were still quite capable of being distractible, and stubborn about focusing again.

Filan raised up on her back legs, pushing her broad head into Thora's palm. Pointedly reminding Thora that while *Derwyn* ranged ahead after those silly fluttering birds, *Filan* was right by her side, doing what she was supposed to.

Watching out for threats. Keeping her eyes and nose out for game. And checking for traces of the PureHuman settlement that was supposed to be out here.

"Yes, you're a good big kitty," Thora said under her breath, rubbing Filan's head. "I expect you'd be off like a shot if a raccoon ran in front of us, but we won't worry about that right now."

Both Filan and Derwyn stood with their backs as high as Thora's knee, and they could easily reach her waist when they stretched. Her hand covered the tops of their massive heads, but not by much. Their huge, rumbling purrs were wonderful to go to sleep to.

Derwyn came loping back, his long tail held high enough for Thora to grab it. He turned and rubbed his mouth against her leg, then he butted heads with Filan.

They were a matched set and fast friends, but breeding was not an option for either of them. Thora had taken them in from illegal breeding rings, like many of her fellow gen-modded humans often did. But she'd ended the line as far as hers were concerned. Both of her cats were sterile.

For exactly the same reason she was.

After widespread genetic modification of humans accidentally left vast numbers vulnerable to the *malance*—a lethal, fast-moving disease that wiped out eighty percent of the world's population over ten years ago if her count was right—everyone left alive got real paranoid, real fast.

The birth of GenSec led quickly to the death of a hell of a lot of people, animals, and plants, with no chance for study or discussion or appeal.

Thora caught the scent and heard the rustle only a split second after her cats did, another sign of her own mods to go along with her hair.

She reached down and clicked the extra-heavy leads onto their harnesses just in case.

"I'm unarmed," she called, clipping the leads onto her own thick belt and holding her hands high. "Only me and two cats, both secured."

The rustles got louder in front of her, the source hidden by a thicket of shiny-leaved rhododendrons.

Both cats growled loud and low.

"I'm not here to steal anything," she said. "I only want to talk to you."

Thora heard the soft pop of the gun and the *whoosh* right before a sharp pain bit into the left side of her chest. She barely had time to see the tiny black tranquilizer pellet—about the length of her thumbnail—before both cats screamed in fury.

"It's okay, babies," she said, sinking through instant mind-fog to her knees, rubbing both of their long backs. They were biting at the same pellets in their own shoulders. "You're just going to go to sleep for a while. I'll be with you."

She settled back onto the ground and into darkness as the cats sat beside her. Thora hoped the tranq dose wasn't too strong for them.

They still growled, but the sound was softer and slower.

"Just hang…hang on," she said, forcing the words out through what felt like a thickening throat. "I'll be with… you. Right there."

She collapsed forward onto the ground, both cats pressing themselves tight against her sides. She couldn't tell if they were still growling or purring or simply trembling.

Footsteps came closer, crunching through the leaves, no longer worried about being quiet.

Thora smelled fear almost as great as her own.

"Don't hurt them," she whispered. "The cats. Please don't…hurt…"

THORA DIDN'T SEEM to have moved when she opened her eyes. She was on her back staring up into the autumn leaves and darkening blue sky above, so that was new. The bumpy, hard dirt of the trail poked into her back and legs. She even felt the warmth of the cats still pressed close against her side.

But when she tried to reach over to check their breathing, she realized her wrists were bound, secured tight against her hips. A quick twitch of her legs let he know her ankles and knees were as well.

"You're trespassing," a woman said from far enough past her head that Thora couldn't see her, in a voice that did not sound the least bit friendly. "You would have been better off staying away. If you're lucky and answer our questions, we'll let you get yourself and your illegal animals turned around and take yourself out of here."

Thora's heart sped up, and sweat broke out on her face. If she made it through this, turning around might be a hell of a lot less scary.

As long as she didn't hold it up against illness and starvation.

"Please, I'm unarmed, just like I said. You can see the cats were on harness. I need to talk to you. You know I never would have been out here otherwise. I know how you feel about us."

After a few endless seconds, two women stepped close enough for her to see. Both were built strong and sturdy, but only to natural human specifications. Both wore clothing similar to Thora's, much cleaner and far better maintained. One with darker brown hair than the other, again, within human specs, and both had skin darker than hers.

"What the hell were you doing out here?" the smaller woman said. She held a gleaming black rifle, pointed at the scrubby undergrowth for now. "If you actually *did* know how we feel about Gen-Mods, you wouldn't be within miles of this place."

Thora nodded, relaxing her hands and arms instead of tensing up like she wanted to. The cats didn't move, but she was pretty sure they were breathing.

"I wouldn't be out here if I wasn't desperate. First thing you need to know is I'm sterilized, and so are the cats. We're not illegals trying to pollute your pure gene pool. We're also starving and need help."

The taller woman stood with her well-muscled arms crossed, but Thora was certain she had weapons close at hand, too.

"You expect us to do *what* about that?" Gun-woman said. "Take you in and feed you? How many other Gen-Mods would follow you right to us? We only have your word that any of you are sterile."

Thora took a deep breath, forcing herself to stay calm. She caught a strong whiff of how scared these two were on the breeze. And that there were several more frightened humans not far behind them.

"There are only seventeen of us. I'm by far the oldest, so I volunteered to come out here to try to find you. We're not going to make it through another winter, not even with the cats helping us hunt."

Gun-woman shrugged, shaking her head.

But Thora was sure a frown of concern crossed the unarmed woman's face.

"Listen, I understand why you don't want us around," Thora said. "But we didn't make the modifications, you *have* to know that. Our grandparents and parents did it, and some of them didn't even want us after we were born. A few of the kids with me were abandoned after they didn't come out matching specifications."

"And your cats?" Gun-woman said. "GenMods were banned long enough ago they shouldn't be alive. It took years to round up enough pure cats and dogs and livestock before they established the preserves so we could start over."

One of the cats (probably Derwyn) twitched against her side, and Thora let out a grunt.

"Yeah, these were bred illegally," she said. "But I took them in rather than letting them suffer and starve. They may look like wildcats, but they're housecats at heart. They can't make it without us. They didn't do anything wrong, either."

The unarmed woman leaned against a smooth-barked tree and spoke for the first time.

"What is it you want from us?"

Gun-woman glared, but she didn't say anything.

"We're settled in a little valley about ten miles from here. Outside the preserve, where GenSec blasted the land to kill all the modded plants and most of the animals. The fruit and vegetable strains we have…they're not pure. I think they're failing, no matter how fast we replace them. We can't find enough animals nearby either. We're starving. We need help."

Unarmed stared at Gun-holder, waiting for her to look back. So Unarmed was clearly a subordinate, but not cowed enough to keep her mouth shut *all* the time.

"I don't see what we could do for you," Gun-woman said, still focused on Thora. "If we send back a load of food and animals, you said it yourself. Where you are was blasted. Your strains aren't failing because you need new ones, or pure ones. The land was intentionally...*spoiled* when GenSec took out all the plants. They made sure nothing would grow outside of the preserves for decades to come."

Thora's guts twisted and she felt a tear run from her eye down toward her ear.

"Are you sure? I never heard that in any of the 'casts."

Gun-woman shook her head.

"You wouldn't have. GenSec was trying to make sure none of the modded plant strains or fungus or insects or anything else would keep spreading and infect everything. That never made it out to the public broadcasts. The only reason we knew about it inside the preserves was so we wouldn't try to get soil or plants from outside. That's all."

Thora drew in a deep breath, not sure what she was going to say until she opened her mouth.

"That's *not* all! I just told you people are starving and nothing will grow. We didn't cause this any more than you did. Everyone who did is long dead, but you're just going to stand there and let us join them when you could stop it?"

She stopped to catch her breath, trying to keep the tears from stealing her voice.

"Even if you don't shoot me and leave me out here to rot, you'll be murderers. If you refuse to help us when you know what's going on, you're worse than the old GenModders. They had the excuse of not knowing what would happen. *You* know."

Gun-woman finally blinked and turned aside, looking toward the river.

"When it happened," she said, "when GenSec decided to blast and spoil everything, they told us there were no people left out there. That GenMods—you—had all died from your mods, been killed by the *malance*, or you'd been rounded up and taken to settlement areas. By the time any of us found out GenSec was lying, it was too late. The damage had already been done all over North America and everywhere else."

Thora closed her eyes and all the energy seemed to drain out of her body.

No wonder everything they tried to do failed.

"There are so many of us out there. Less than twenty in our camp right now, but I've been traveling since the whole thing started to fall apart, since the first *malance* outbreaks. I've met hundreds and heard about *thousands* who went underground. We all knew to hide in a preserve or get into a cave when the blasts hit. That part of the plan wasn't nearly as secret as GenSec thought."

She opened her eyes and met Unarmed's gaze.

"Apparently the fact that any of us are alive at all was the biggest secret."

The cat on Thora's other side twitched, giving her the faintest sliver of hope. If the cats were alive, at least she could keep on going for a while. She hadn't let them down, not yet.

Unarmed leaned close to Gun-woman, speaking in a low voice. They probably had no idea how keen Thora's modded hearing truly was.

"You can't just leave them out there to starve. We all know what happened was wrong, what GenSec did. Now we know they lied to everyone inside *and* outside the preserves. Are we really going to repeat their mistakes when there aren't enough of *us* left, either?"

"And if all the damned mods get right back into our genomes?" Gun-woman said. "As hard as everyone worked to try to find clean lines and keep them that way? We'd lose everything we've been fighting for."

Thora decided some secrets were more valuable when she stopped hiding them.

"I'm already sterile," she said, not surprised when her captors jumped and stared at her. "By surgery years ago, but I would have been by simple old age a lot more recently. I'm no threat to you. Neither are these cats."

Unarmed walked closer, glancing at the cats before she looked into Thora's eyes.

"That's one of your mods?" she said. "Hearing?"

She nodded, the back of her head shifting over the dirt. Being honest about this part was a hell of a lot harder when talking to one PureHuman while another angry one stood close by, but she had to take her chance while any of them were actually listening to her.

"Hearing, sense of smell. Purple hair for some insane reason no one ever quite explained to me, but I do remember almost all the kids my age having strange hair colors when I was in school. If my family was telling me the truth, I might have an extended life span despite my biological clock running down a few years back. Assuming I don't starve to death first."

Unarmed rubbed at her chin, then looked at the cats again.

"Do they have anything other than size?"

Gun-woman stepped closer. "What's the point of this?"

"The point is we're having trouble too, Mavi. That and I'm never going to like the idea of murder after what GenSec did. They told us there were *no* humans out there when the blast hit, remember?"

Thora waited until they finished glaring at each other and looked at her.

"I don't know as much about the cats, since they were basically rescued from an illegal breeding ring. I've had them for about three years. They seem more...responsive than most housecats. Calmer. Able to walk on a leash, stay close when we're out like this. But they're housecats through and through otherwise. Sweet and silly and sometimes shy, jumping at their own shadows and braver than they should be. They'll streak off like lunatics if they see a bird or some other kind of prey in their path."

Gun-Woman—Mavi— squatted beside Thora's shoulder, still keeping her eyes on the cats. Both of them twitched against Thora's sides now, like they were caught in a vivid dream.

"How do you know that?" she said. "That's the second time you mentioned them hunting. What can they be finding out there?"

Thora took a deep breath, trying to find a way to say it without antagonizing the person she most needed on her side.

"They mostly hunted each other when they were kittens, just like any other cat. Now, the boundaries of the preserves aren't solid. Animals cross over the same way people do. And animals managed to hide out underground like we did, too."

Mavi closed her eyes and shook her head, and Thora was afraid her words had gotten too close to her thoughts.

But what *were* she and the cats if not proof that living things were still outside the preserves?

"That's not…what GenSec led us to believe," Mavi said slowly. "We knew the borders were open, of course. They were built in sheltered areas like this one, areas that should have kept the animals inside where they had food, and it pretty much has. But they told us all the animals were gone outside. From the *malance* or the blast."

"Just like they said about people," Unarmed said. She watched Thora for a few seconds. "Do you need to sit up?"

"If I can. My back isn't doing great on the dirt here. The

cats are twitching like they're about to wake, so don't be startled if they do."

Unarmed-woman squatted on the other side of Thora, and she and Mavi lifted her up by her shoulders. They then scooted her backward to a broad oak tree so she could lean against it. The cats rolled bonelessly toward each other until they were side by side

"Thank you," Thora said. "My name is Thora. The black male is Derwyn, the tabby female is Filan. They normally would never think of hurting you, but they may try if they think you're hurting me."

"I'm Erin, and I already slipped up with Mavi's name." She took a couple of steps away from Thora and the cats before she squatted again. "Do you have other domestic animals? Others that hunt and share with you? We have dogs that hunt the—"

"Don't you think that's enough, Erin?" Mavi said. She still stood, and she still held her rifle. "Until today we thought we were alone out here. We have no way to know if she's telling us the truth yet. We shouldn't be telling her anything, much less everything."

Thora opened her mouth to protest, then stopped. None of this was helping. She had the feeling Mavi would talk her in circles until all of them got tired of it and gave up.

Then they'd all walk away, assuming they even bothered to untie her.

"Then let's go see for ourselves," Erin said. "What they have isn't working and what *we* have isn't working. GenSec collapsed along with everything else a long time ago. I don't happen to love the idea of sitting here in our little preserve and dying out anyway. A pure genome can go every bit as extinct as a modded one."

Derwyn predictably picked that moment to raise his head, breathing in several times before letting loose with a tremendous growling yawn. He staggered to his feet, shaking his head.

Mavi twitched her gun up several inches.

"No, please," Thora said, leaning forward. "He's just confused. Let him wake up and find me. Derwyn, I'm right here."

He turned in a circle, still unsteady on his feet, then blinked his huge green eyes several times in her direction. He gave a mournful sounding low-pitched yowl and lurched toward her.

"Is he hurt?" Erin said.

"I think he's confused," Thora said. "He has no idea what happened. Is so much dizziness normal with the tranq you shot us with?"

Derwyn collapsed against Thora's leg, rubbing his face against her thigh and yowling again.

Mavi looked down and kicked at the leaves underfoot, her cheeks turning red.

"I don't know for sure. I've never used one on an animal. Only a couple of other people besides you."

"Listen, I'm not armed," Thora said. She looked down at the matte gray bindings that still held her hands against her hips and wrapped around her thighs, knees, and ankles. "And I'm not going anywhere with my legs bound. Can you please untie me so I can make sure he's okay?"

Instead of looking to Mavi as she had the whole time, Erin moved to a half-crouch and closed the distance to Thora's side, watching Derwyn. The cat tried to focus on the movement but his eyes kept tracking off to the side.

Thora barely managed to keep herself from laughing when Derwyn let out another awful yowl and Erin jumped. She was glad she hadn't laughed when Erin held a small black device near one of her hands. When it let out a high-pitched whirring noise, the bindings loosened immediately.

Thora held both of her empty, tingling hands up for the two women to see, then leaned toward Derwyn.

"Hey there big kitty." She let him sniff her hands, then rubbed the sides of his mouth and the top of his head. He was drooling horribly. "Looks like you're feeling sick. I'm right here, Derwyn Doof. You'll feel better soon."

The awful sliding movement of his eyes was starting to slow down, but he still couldn't look at Thora. He yowled again, but not as loud or as pitiful.

"He seems to be getting better," Thora said. "Hopefully it's wearing off."

"Will someone be coming after you?" Mavi said. She still held the gun, but it was again pointed at the ground. "If you don't get back at a certain time?"

Thora shook her head. Filan stretched out one front leg, then the others.

"They don't really know where I was headed," she said. "I was only going by what I remembered about a park here years ago. With the high mountains around the protected valley, it made sense to head this way. We'd heard there was a settlement, but nothing else about it."

Erin sat cross-legged on the remnants of the trail a good distance from Filan.

"So they'll just give you up for dead?" she said. "If you don't come back?"

"They won't have much choice. I didn't tell them where I was headed. The thinking is I'm the oldest with the most experience at surviving and the most skills and memories. If something kills me, it *will* kill them. Anyway, we're used to people disappearing and dying. We don't know anything else."

Filan raised her head then, and flopped it right back down. Rather than Derwyn's sad yowl, she gave out urgent, groaning, high meows, one after the other.

"This way, sweet girl," Thora called. "Come up here to me. You'll feel better in a minute."

"Should I...try to help her?" Mavi said, surprising Thora with the worried tone of her voice. "They almost sound like babies."

"They're just like any hurt or confused creature," Thora said. "I'm not sure what she'll do, but she's never intentionally hurt a person. You can try letting her smell your hand, then see if she'll let you pick her up. Support her head, like you would a baby's."

Mavi raised her eyebrows, but she stepped forward.

"I've never picked up a baby with teeth and claws like that. Help me, Erin?"

After carefully sniffing both women's hands, Filan resumed her heartbreaking meows. It took a few false starts and jerking back, but they finally got the cat half-dragged, half-carried across the leaves and dirt to Thora's side.

When Filan got a sniff of Thora's hand, she meowed one last time, holding the sound as long as she could and ending up in a growl. Derwyn rumbled in return, finally managing to focus on Thora's face when she scratched the top of his head.

"Thank you. I think they'll stay calm until they feel better. I feel better too, knowing they're okay."

Thora was surprised to see Erin and even Mavi blinking back tears, though she wouldn't have been with any of the people she'd spent the last several years with. Modded humans had an easier time understanding these were nothing more than larger versions of housecats.

"I'm sorry I tranqed them," Mavi said. "And you. I'll probably sound just like the PureHuman asshole you think I am, but I'm not sure what going to your settlement would accomplish. It could be an ambush, Erin."

"Like we ambushed *her*, you mean?" Erin said. "An

unarmed person walking toward us, asking us for help? The first person *any* of us has ever seen from outside the preserve?"

Thora clenched her teeth, forcing herself to keep silent. All she could do was make the dispute between the two of them worse, and hurt her own cause in the process.

Mavi's features hardened. "You know the risks, *both* of you. The *malance* didn't go away. It could easily sweep through what's left of us if their modded weakness gets back in."

Erin stood abruptly and kicked at the oak tree Thora was leaning against, making both cats jump. Derwyn's wide-pupil gaze locked onto her, but Filan's head only swayed before she pushed her face hard against Thora's leg.

"No, it didn't go away," Erin said, walking past Thora's feet. "But doesn't the fact that people obviously survived the *malance* and the blast and everything else mean anything to you? These are human beings, Mavi, modded or not. In case you haven't noticed, there aren't that many of us let anywhere."

Mavi got up herself, and stared up at the bright autumn leaves, at the sky deepening toward the indigo of night.

"It's getting late," she said. "And cold. We couldn't get to your settlement tonight anyway if it's as far away as you say. When did you last see any signs of the *malance*, Thora? In your group or any other?"

"Not since the big wave years ago. Ten years, I think, but I'm not sure. We think all the vulnerable ones got wiped out by it then. A whole lot more people than either side could stand to lose have died since then, but not of the *malance*."

For the first time since Thora saw her, Mavi swung the rifle strap over her shoulder and twisted it around to her back. Out of her reach. She crossed her arms and looked at Erin, then back at Thora.

"Either you haven't said or I wasn't listening, but what did you come here for? What did you want from us?"

A bitter laugh escaped before Thora could stop it.

"What we wanted, or at least what we hoped for, was healthier strains of plants. Something I could take back and we could grow on our own. That way we wouldn't trouble you again, and we hoped you'd let us be as long as we stayed away. But healthy plants wouldn't do us any good at all, would they?"

Mavi shook her head. "Not for very long, and maybe not for a long time. GenSec thought things would start to regrow by now, twelve years by our count. Sounds like you're not seeing any signs of that yet."

"Not in our food crops. Or natural trees or grasses. I've heard of modded flowers and fruit springing up closer to the old cities, though. I guess they were tougher than GenSec thought. Just like us."

Erin slowly walked over to Mavi's side, Derwyn's gaze following her every step of the way.

"We can't leave them out here, Mavi. We don't know how long that tranq will take to wear off, especially with the cats. There are animals out here that won't show any mercy once the sun goes down."

"Okay then," Mavi said, stepping close to Thora. "You're taking the risk here, probably more than we are. What do you think we should do?"

"You're right, we can't make it back to our settlement, not tonight. Why don't you blindfold me and take me to *your* settlement? I won't know any more than I do now. You can keep me in one spot there if you want as long as the cats are with me so they won't get upset. Then tomorrow morning blindfold me again, and we head out."

Erin squatted beside Thora again, cautiously holding her

knuckles out toward Derwyn. He sniffed her thoroughly, then rubbed his mouth across her hand.

"You don't care that we'll know where you live?" Erin said smiling as she rubbed the huge cat's head. "That we'd be able to find you?"

Thora shrugged. "We're going to starve before winter's over. It might be quicker and less painful if you kill us instead."

Mavi winced and rubbed her hands together. The chill rose up from the ground under Thora's backside and came down from the air.

"Okay. It's getting dark anyway. I can't make any kind of promises about what will happen if we take you with us. There are some people your age who are *not* going to understand us bringing you there. But Erin's right, and so are you. At least the two of us can't leave you out here to starve."

"They might change their minds once they know people survived the blast," Erin said. She leaned forward and loosened the bindings around Thora's legs. "I'll do everything I can to make sure they do."

Thora shifted and stretched her legs, getting grumbles and answering stretches from the cats. Filan was finally able to focus on Thora, and she reached down to scratch the huge M on her broad forehead.

She didn't say it out loud, but she was afraid anyone her age or older already *knew* modded humans had survived the blast. After all, people that same age at GenSec had planned and authorized the blast in the first place, and whatever had fouled the soil for years.

But if she didn't wasn't willing to take this chance, grasp at this fragile bit of hope, she would be just as cynical and fatalistic as they must have been.

She took one each of Mavi's and Erin's hands and slowly got to her feet. Filan and Derwyn stood and stretched, tails high and waving in the air, front claws flexing and digging into the dirt and leaves. Thora reached down and made sure the leads between her belt and the cats' harnesses were secure.

"Think the cats will be able to walk another couple of miles?" Mavi said. "Will *you* be?"

Thora leaned back with her hands in the small of her back for her own stretch. Her feet hurt, sure, and her hips and knees protested the rising chill and damp.

But for the first time in years, she was going to be walking *toward* something instead of running away in hopes she'd keep breathing.

"We could walk all night long if the chance to live another day was at the end of it. We're ready."

WICKED BONE

KARI KILGORE

AUTHOR OF SONGS IN THE MOUNTAIN & IN THE PINES

For Loretta

My very own Pashmina.

CHAPTER 1

THE BRIGHT WHITE ceramic tiles in the glorious, airy sunroom were one of Katie's favorite things about the vacation house high in the Virginia Blue Ridge Mountains. Light flooded in from three glass walls and the ceiling, making this one of the few places she felt truly warm so far north in the deep wintertime.

The angular, Art Deco lounge chairs and loveseat had matching white steel frames contrasted with deep, thick cushions in luscious, cheerful shades of every hue she loved. Blue, red, green, purple, and especially pink transformed the room from a beautiful if sterile white box into her little slice of personal heaven.

Even on painfully, unreasonably frigid days, the intense sunlight let Katie pursue her lifelong art and passion of gardening. Rich, earthy scents of jasmine and patchouli brought a welcome touch of her pride and joy, her sprawling prize-winning garden in Miami, to their frozen northern retreat.

The peppery bite of nasturtium lingered on her tongue. She couldn't resist munching on at least one of the gorgeous orange flowers every time she set foot in her Garden of Eden North. Thanks to Nora, their neighbor and caretaker while they were out of town, Katie's plants were always thriving.

Brilliant, marriage-saving compromises with her long-time husband Ken stretched far past her beloved white tile and rainbow of cushions in one spectacular room. Ken was out here as often as she was, enjoying the endless sea of mountains, blue and green and brown rolling and swelling as far as the eye could see in warmer weather.

Today crashing waves of brilliant white set off a soaring winter sky so blue it made Katie's eyes water. Well-planned and expensive construction paid off as the high altitude wind picked up. Glittering veils of ice diamonds danced across her view and over the transparent roof, bringing whispery sounds like sand skittering across the beach. Not the slightest trace of chilly air intruded no matter how hard that bitter wind tried to force its way in.

The house itself was a grand compromise, one Katie was thankful they'd come to the year she'd turned forty-five and Ken forty-three. She would have preferred a house further south than their home in Miami, maybe even the hedonistic, rum-soaked paradise of Key West. She still held out hope for that cozy, exclusive bungalow where the ghost of Hemmingway roamed free as the chickens.

Ken longed for the mountains of his childhood, though, and she had to admit he was right about the song and beauty of the rugged land. At the height of smothery, muggy summer in Florida, the cool breezes and chorus of frogs and insects up here were a symphony for her senses.

A soft, tickly caress across her bare feet, warmed by the fabulous radiant floor heating, reminded Katie of another much-loved compromise. She picked up a delicate, soft as cashmere, absolutely stunning solid black cat. Pashmina rumbled like she had a belly full of bumblebees, and she blinked her gorgeous deep green eyes slow as sweat rolling down a huge glass of summer afternoon iced tea.

Katie had never been a pet person until those emerald beauties claimed ownership of her heart as surely as Ken had.

"Glad to be back in the mountains, my Pashmina love?"

She held the dainty creature up to her ear, grinning as the purrs vibrated through her own skull. Pashmina batted at Katie's brown curls, then tried to pull her reading glasses from the top of her head.

"You're right, gorgeous girl. Mommy did come out here to do a little reading."

Katie headed toward her escapist and adventure corner, a huge purple beanbag piled high with rainbow pillows, and the delightful fantasy adventure novel she'd been dying to get back to. She loved anything but legal thrillers. Her real life job as an attorney made it far too clear that courtrooms were much more hurry up and wait than anything thrilling.

Before she took three steps, she froze.

There. Right there on her perfect, clean white tile.

Once in a great while, deep down inside her own mind, Katie remembered why she'd never wanted pets in the first place.

A smear of blood. A tiny fluff of grey fur.

A stomach no bigger than a dime.

Katie groaned. "*Why* can't you wait until Ken gets home?"

Pashmina blinked her seductive, languorous blink and purred even louder.

Katie put the vicious, murderous feline on the dark red loveseat. Appropriate match for such horrifying bloodlust.

"Good kitty," Katie said under her breath. Ken said she had to praise Pashmina for her excellent hunting feats, no matter how messy or how often. "Brave kitty. Clever girl."

Pashmina rolled onto her back, but Katie had finally

learned not to fall for that trap. Cat requests for a belly rub came with claws and sometimes teeth right behind.

The ways of the tiny house panther's hunts were still foreign and mysterious to Katie, and she thought they always would be. One day a delicate, pathetic foot lingered to announce the kill.

Another day, the tail. A head without a body. A body without a head.

In Florida Pashmina added lizards, huge insects, and an occasional scorpion to her menu, but continued her rejection of some random body part. Always proudly displayed where Katie would be sure to notice. No rhyme or reason to any of it.

Only bleach and gloves and scrubbing.

CHAPTER 2

JUST AS KATIE stepped out into the gusting wind cutting through her indoor clothes like a hand through still water, she heard the jangling approach of Ken's Jeep. He'd bought a second-hand dark blue boxy monstrosity, outfitted with four wheel drive and pulleys and winches and everything else he could think up.

That was another idea of his that seemed strange to her at first, but it shifted into perfect sense and clarity after the first snowstorm up here.

The Jeep still looked horrid to Katie, and her ears recoiled from the irritating noise of the chains on the quiet winter day. And she was consistently amazed at how well that sturdy tank made it through the worst that winter or spring storms could throw at it. So far no creek was too flooded, no road too muddy, and no snow drift too high to stop Ken and his favorite mountain toy retrieved from his childhood.

She dropped the bag of distasteful guts and the paper towels she'd used to clean it into one of their three huge garbage cans. Ken was returning from hauling off the garbage among other things, so the small paper sack made a massive resounding thunk in the empty green canister. The frigid air damped down the musty, rotten smell that lingered no matter how clean the inside of the cans looked.

Katie flipped the raccoon guard—a bar that covered all three cans and kept their garbage inside rather than scattered all over the ground—down just as Ken's Jeep rounded the last curve of their steep graveled road.

He tapped the old-fashioned blaring horn once, and she heard the rough motor grind down into a lower gear. They left the grouchy old mountain goat here year-round, thank goodness, at her brother-in-law Dave's rustic cabin lower down the mountain. Her sensible and lovely grey Volvo waited in town for the return journey to warmer surroundings.

Katie couldn't imagine trying to make it to Georgia, much less all the way down the length of Florida, on those jouncy Jeep seats with plastic windows shrieking in her ears. She doubted the stubborn thing would make it to highway speeds even going down the miles-long mountain toward North Carolina.

"Hey there gorgeous!" Ken said as he pushed the Jeep's screechy door open. "What the hell are you doing out here in the cold?"

Katie realized her teeth were chattering, making her skull and her jaw ache.

"I heard you coming for the last three miles," she said, smiling without exposing her sensitive teeth to the awful cold. "I decided you deserved a hero's welcome for hauling the garbage away with your trusty battle-hardened steed there."

Ken leaned back in and grabbed two canvas grocery bags off the front seat. He wore a plaid-lined denim jacket and a goofy red wool cap with the ear flaps pulled down, both hand-me-downs from his grandfather. Katie couldn't see his red hair shot through with silver under the hat, but his mountain man beard only had a little bit of color left in it. She knew he'd shave every trace of it before they drove south, no matter how many times she said he looked more rugged and manly with whiskers, gray or not.

"I return to you in triumph, my Lady," he said, leaning down with a cold, bristly kiss. "Having dispatched the foul midden pit and secured wondrous feasts for our fair household."

"Bring them inside posthaste before they freeze solid, my Lord." Katie checked for a lurking Pashmina before she opened the glass kitchen door. Despite her pampered indoor life and variety of hunting conquests, the cat still sometimes tried to dart outside whenever they were here. "I'll start a fire to thaw all of us out."

"Seriously, why were you out there?" Ken said, hanging his coat and hat on the row of hooks by the door. His hair crackled with static. "It's just above zero."

Katie grimaced before she could help herself.

"Pashmina secured her own wondrous feast. She left me the most choice morsels, as usual."

Ken wrinkled his nose and caught her up in a proper, surprisingly warm hug.

"What bit did she leave this time? In the sunroom again?"

"Of course in the sunroom," Katie said, breathing in the wool and sweat and firewood scent of her husband. "She can't resist blood on white tile. The stomach most foul displeased Her Majesty today."

"I wish you'd leave that for me." Ken kissed her cheek and turned to help her put the groceries away.

Katie shuddered. "I can't stand to leave it all over the floor. I just wish I knew why she does this. The different bits, I mean."

"Because she loves you?" Ken winked as he opened the black refrigerator. "My brother actually reminded me today of what our grandmother used to say about things like this. Granny said every creature on God's Earth was born with a wicked bone."

"Every creature?" Katie stowed a bag of small red potatoes in their bin and turned back to him. "That sounds a bit extreme."

"Well, she did make an exception for whatever dogs she had at the time. Especially the redbone hounds. They were exempt. But every other critter had a wicked bone. Could be muscles or guts or whatever, and cats wouldn't eat that part. She said if they ate the wicked parts, they'd get too evil and mean to live around people."

"Not a cat person, huh?"

"My Granny? Not even a little bit. But she always had one to deal with the mice no one can keep control of out here. They were always black, too, just like your killer princess there. Maybe Pashmina knows how heartbroken you'd be if she turned all nasty on you."

Katie glanced toward the sunroom, and dark green eyes were indeed watching her. Pashmina sat in the doorway with her bushy, luxurious tail curled around her feet, giving every appearance of listening in.

"She's right about that," Katie said. She made the kissy noises her house panther loved, and Pashmina wrapped like liquid velvet around her ankles. "I wonder if it offends her when I throw them out."

Ken laughed. "Well, you won't be surprised to hear my Granny held firm beliefs on the matter. She said you had to get rid of whatever a cat left you, and right quick. That's one reason she hated it when folks around here started embalming humans instead of burying them right away. Remember how fast her funeral was?"

"I couldn't possibly forget. I had to cancel with an incredibly unsympathetic judge to make it up here in time."

"I appreciate that still." Ken kissed the tip of her nose. "Granny flat-out refused, made sure it was in her will that she would not be embalmed. She insisted on going in the ground quick even though she despised graveyards, so she could turn to dust straightaway. She was always onto us to never hang around or play in them, especially the big modern ones. All those wicked bones gathered up and preserved forever."

"So humans have wicked bones, too?"

Ken grunted. "Usually a lot more than one bone. You know that better than anyone, Madame Prosecutor. Wicked humans all over Florida are a big part of what paid for this little chalet."

CHAPTER 3

MORE THAN A DECADE of charmed winter travel luck disappeared when Katie and Ken, and Pashmina, returned for the holidays a month later. Even the valiant and much-maligned Jeep didn't stand a chance against several huge oak trees down across the road after a windy blizzard.

The original family homestead cabin could not have been a sharper contrast from the high-tech modern chalet. The few windows were low and small, but upgraded insulation and smooth, sheetrock walls let only a few drafts roar through. Once Katie bundled up in a scarf, sweater, and thick socks, she couldn't deny the charm of their temporary location while they waited for an overburdened road crew to arrive.

Her brother-in-law Dave kept fires roaring in a wood stove on each floor, and the spiced wine on top of the soapstone model downstairs provided a delightful welcoming smell and delicious warm treat. Katie and Pashmina set up housekeeping on the overstuffed sectional sofa near the fire downstairs, while Ken and Dave competed to see who could bring in the biggest armload of firewood.

With a stack of novels at the ready and a warm, rumbly

cat on her lap or curled up close to the wood stove, Katie had to admit this might be a tradition well worth repeating on future visits.

That cozy sense of family togetherness lasted until she realized just how many more mice could sneak in through the walls of the hundred-thirty-year-old cabin, modernized or not. And how much Pashmina enjoyed sharpening her claws and her hunting skills upon them.

The first catch seemed innocent enough. On the first night, with Ken and Dave both on their phones trying to track down anyone who could clear the massive trees, Pashmina dashed across the floor in front of Katie. She crouched in front of the fire, then batted a rounded shape from the thick blue hearth rug onto the dark, scarred hardwood floor.

A shape that moved and sounded like a plastic milk lid, one of the feline princess's less distressing toys.

A shape that seemed oddly brown and furry. Surely that was a trick of low light and travel weary eyes.

Both men were still in the small, bright yellow kitchen, pacing and talking into their mobile phones. Neither of them were smiling, so Katie decided to investigate herself. As was often the case when it came to her precious and puzzling dainty black cat, Katie regretted her curiosity immediately.

Pashmina jumped into her lap at the usual kissy sounds, silky tail high and waving her backside in Katie's face.

"What have you found, you spoiled rotten creature?"

The cat turned and dropped her treasure onto the clean white pages of Katie's latest science fiction mystery.

A perfectly preserved, lifelike, mummified mouse.

If Dave had a fireplace instead of the stove, she would have thrown the whole thing, book and all, into the flames. Instead she groaned and put the book, the mouse, and the cat on the paisley cushion beside her.

"Everything okay in there?" Ken said from the kitchen door. He still held his phone to his ear.

"No, not really. This vicious creature found... I don't even want to say."

Dave walked through the other kitchen door at her words, muttering into his own handset. He was a nearly perfect duplicate of his older brother, only with silvery black hair instead of red and a year-round beard. His uniform of flannel shirts over t-shirts, blue jeans, and hiking boots were year-round, too.

"Great, thank you," Dave said into the phone. "They'll be at my place. Call me if anything changes. What's wrong, Katie?"

She stood and pointed at the horrible thing. Right in the middle of her brand new book.

Dave stepped closer, scowling, then he picked up the mouse. In his bare hands.

"Wow, this must have been behind the stove," he said, holding it by the stiffened tail. "I haven't seen one like this in years."

"Nora says the power is still on, her place and ours," Ken said, standing beside Katie. "She'll check again tomorrow. Hey, a mouse mummy. I remember these from when Granny still lived here. Did Pashmina find it?"

"Yes, that cat found it," Katie said. She sat and held up her book to the bright lamp hanging over her shoulder and blew to get rid of any lingering fur. "She was batting it around like a toy."

Ken sat next to her, and to his credit, he was only smiling a little.

"Look at it this way, Sweetheart." He kissed her cheek. "Maybe she won't bring you the usual bits and pieces if she has this. You know, the fresh ones."

Dave put the mouse on the hardwood and pushed with

his fingertips. Pashmina pounced before it went more than a few inches. She trotted into the kitchen with the bizarre prize in her mouth, long black hair flouncing with her steps, growling the whole way.

"I'll pay you to keep us in mouse mummies if this works," Katie said.

A tiny gray tail curled up in her slipper in the middle of the night, not the least bit mummified, showed Katie how long Pashmina could hold up her end of the macabre bargain.

CHAPTER 4

THE NEXT DAY started off cold, clear, and with fresh wicked bone remainders in different parts of the cabin, all proudly arranged for best visibility and effect. Katie didn't hesitate to let Ken and Dave handle the cleanup and the requisite enthusiastic praise for her murdering beast.

She'd heard how cats had an unerring sense of who didn't want their attention at the moment, and Pashmina did spend every second as close to Katie as she could get. Or at least as close as Katie allowed with the eerily lifelike mouse mummy in constant attendance.

"Now you see why I have all the food in storage bins down here," Dave said, closing the front door. He dropped a huge armload of wood into the rack beside the stove, then leaned down to pet the source of so much slaughter. "Thank you, pretty girl. Maybe I need to get a couple of cats of my own to keep up her good work."

"Ken said your grandmother always kept a black one," Katie said. "Like this little murderer here."

"Oh yeah, this place was overrun with mice and snakes and everything else before I closed up the walls a bit. She let her cats outside sometimes, but they kept plenty busy in here."

"Snakes?" Katie said. "That's one of the few things she hasn't caught in Florida yet. I guess that means they can't get in the house, thank goodness. Do snakes have wicked bones?"

Dave laughed as he sat in his usual giant recliner close to the stove.

"A whole lot of folks say snakes are the original wicked bone, don't they?" Pashmina abandoned Katie and jumped onto his lap, mouse and all. "I figure snakes are working hard to eat up the mice, too."

"I never let this wretched demon outside," Katie said. "She does enough damage indoors."

"Granny didn't let 'em out often, afraid they'd catch the songbirds. She was strange about it, too." He scratched at his beard, staring into the fire. "I'd always hear her muttering to herself right before, but she never would tell me what was going on. I crept up behind her once, and I would have sworn I heard her say something like 'Get on out there and earn your keep. You best come back a cat.'"

A blast of cold air and low voices followed Ken into the house before Katie could ask what on earth that meant. A man Katie had never seen before was with him, smaller and more wiry than anyone in her husband's family. His face was clean-shaven, unusual in the winter in the mountains, but otherwise not all that remarkable.

"Katie, Dave, this is Jay Bishop," Ken said. He let Katie take the packages and bundles in his arms, results of a last-minute online holiday shopping binge. "He's on his way up to check on Nora's folks on the other side of the mountain. He should be able to clear our road tomorrow."

"Glad to do it," Jay said. "Gonna be up that way anyway, might as well take care of y'all while I'm at it. I can haul that wood back down here once the roads are all clear, stack it up for next winter."

His voice was soft and his accent was strange to Katie's ears, slower and more drawling than her in-laws. A cluster of three bright blue stones glittered from his right earlobe, same color as his eyes. Again, pierced ears on men wasn't unheard of even in the mountains these days. But the earring itself was striking enough to catch her attention.

"Happy to meet you, Jay," Dave said, reaching out to shake Jay's hand. "Even more happy you're in the tree clearing business. I'll sure take you up on the firewood. But I guess it should go up to their house since it's their road blocked."

"We'll split it with you," Ken said, clapping his brother on the back. "Least we can do for you putting up with us. Just let us know when it's cleared, Jay, and we'll settle up."

"I'll sure do that," Jay said. He nodded at all three of them right before he stepped out the door. "I thank you."

"How did you find him?" Dave said. All three of them filed into the kitchen to refill coffee and get lunch ready. "Everyone I called last night was booked solid."

"Yeah, me too," Ken said. "I heard him talking to someone else at the post office about heading up the mountain. I knew if I didn't find someone fast, we'd be stuck here for another week under your feet."

"You're good company, pretty much," Dave said. "Especially if it means firewood for next year. Pashmina's not quite finished clearing the place out for me yet."

Katie watched the silky animal pacing back and forth over the poor, petrified mouse. Pashmina growled every time she got close to the husked out creature. She finally stopped and hunched down in her familiar pounce mode, the front of her body low, wriggling rear high with her tail waving. The cat jumped toward her distressing toy, snatched it up, and ran into the bathroom.

That night, Pashmina finally disposed of her mouse mummy. Everything vanished except the feather-light head proudly displayed in the middle of the bathtub.

She also started the determined habit of sneaking outside that would shatter Katie's understanding of reality forever.

CHAPTER 5

No matter how carefully Katie, Ken, Dave, or anyone else checked before they opened the door, Pashmina managed to dart through and away. She didn't go far at first, at least not while the snow was still on the ground. By the time Katie and Ken got back to their house and muddy yard, the cat stayed out longer every time.

"She can't keep this up in Miami," Katie said when they were in bed on Christmas Eve. Pashmina was curled up on her belly, rumbling and content. "A gator will get her."

"Or a car. We may have to block her into certain rooms. I don't want to scare you, but there are plenty of critters here that could hurt a small cat like this."

"I know." Katie stroked the soft fur, crackling with static in the dry air. "Hawks and bobcats and stray dogs. Are there mountain lions still? Like the panthers in Florida?"

She felt Ken shaking his head.

"Not anymore. They got hunted out almost a hundred years ago. Nothing but rumors of people letting pet ones loose, but nothing ever comes of it. She's safe from that much up here."

Katie scratched under the cat's chin, smiling at how she tilted her head back and forth to exactly the right spot.

"Just like everything else," she said, "I wish I knew *why* she's doing this."

But Pashmina didn't even try to get out when they returned to Florida after New Year's Eve. She settled back into her usual routine of hunting what came into the house and only halfheartedly watching the door.

The frequency of bloody offerings returned to normal, too. Katie hadn't realized until then how much they'd dropped off with the house panther's forays into the outdoors.

Their spring getaway in the mountains, and renewed feline escapes, had her wishing for the typical cat trophies after the first night.

Katie walked into the bright sunroom, mind on an upcoming trial, eyes on the first pinkish blush in the hardwood trees all around them.

She nearly stepped on a shriveled and twisted index finger.

When a soft tickle caressed her ankle, Katie clapped her hand over her mouth to keep from screaming. No mistaking it, and no pretending it was some kind of animal remains. The flesh was wrinkled into grayish leather, the long fingernail coated in dirt.

Pashmina slinked toward the horrible relic. Katie grabbed her and held her against her chest.

"Where did you get that?" she whispered, frozen to the spot. "You can't possibly be digging up graves now."

She backed up, clutching at the purring cat and unable to look away from the thing on the white tile.

At least there was no blood.

Katie misdialed several times before she managed to dial Ken's mobile. Pashmina continued to purr, eyes closed. She kneaded Katie's shoulder, one foot, then the other, over and over.

"Hey sweetheart," Ken said on a miraculously clear connection. "What's up?"

"Can you come home now, please?" Katie said. Her voice trembled in time with her heartbeat. "If Dave's with you, bring him too."

"What's going on, Katie?" Ken sounded stern, his normal response to being scared to death.

"Just hurry, please. Pashmina found something I need your help with. Okay?"

"We'll be right there."

Katie sank onto one of the overstuffed orange chairs beside the window, still staring at the finger. The *human* finger that was somehow inside her house. She only looked away long enough to verify that her sweet, precious cat was sound asleep on the sofa before Ken and Dave stormed into the house barely ten minutes later.

"Katie, thank goodness." Ken knelt beside her. "What's wrong?"

"I think I know," Dave said. He stood over the thing, shaking his head. "When did this show up?"

"Sometime after Ken left," Katie said. "She got out again, so I left the sunroom door cracked like we have been. I don't know when she got back. Where the hell could she even find that?"

"Only thing I can think is one of the old family cemeteries," Dave said. He squatted and stared at the displaced remains. Katie was thankful he didn't pick it up like he had the mouse mummy. "They're scattered through the mountains up here. Doubt anyone knows about them all."

"But aren't the bodies supposed to be buried?" Katie said. "I'm quite sure she didn't dig that up by herself."

"Normally, yeah," Ken said. He squeezed Katie's shoulder, then stood beside his brother. "Something else must have got to this first."

"Should we call someone?" Katie said. "The police, or… I don't know who."

Dave rubbed at his beard, nodding.

"I'll call Sheriff Meade. Even if someone's digging a foundation or something, they need to know what they're actually into."

"Go ahead," Ken said. "I'll take care of this."

Katie wanted to go in the bedroom and lock the door, or maybe lock herself into the bathroom and take a scorching hot shower. But she was afraid if she didn't watch, she'd have nightmares about finding the finger all over the house.

In her shoes. Under her pillow. Inside a box of cereal.

She watched without saying a word while Ken used a pair of her blue kitchen gloves and dropped the shriveled thing into a plastic baggie. When he stepped outside to give the baggie to his brother, still pacing and talking on his phone, Katie got up to grab her bleach. Desiccated or not, she had no desire to wonder if she was stepping on what was left of someone's great-great something or other every time she walked into her sunroom.

When she came back from the kitchen, Pashmina stood on the white tile where she'd left her latest trophy. She'd never seemed to care when Katie got rid of the horrible evidence before. This time she sniffed all around the spot, chirping to herself. Pashmina sneezed, then trotted out of the sunroom.

"Let me do that, hon," Ken said, walking in with Dave right behind him.

"Thank you, but I'll feel better if I do. What did the sheriff say?"

Dave shrugged, shaking his head.

"She doesn't know of anyone digging for a foundation or

a well right now. Sometimes folks work without a permit, though. She's going to come up tomorrow and have a look if that's okay with you."

"Of course it's okay with me." Katie snorted, trying not to breathe in too much of the harsh bleach as she scrubbed. "Even if this slaughter queen wasn't bringing human body parts inside now, I don't like the idea of a bunch of open graves no one knows about."

"You know who we might want to ask," Ken said. "The kid who cleared our road over the winter. Brought us both a bunch of firewood?"

"Yeah, Jay Bishop." Dave had his phone out already, scrolling the screen with his thumb. "He has all the equipment you'd need, bulldozer and backhoe and everything. Seems like a good guy. I'm pretty sure he'd admit it if someone was paying him under the table to work without a permit. Or if he'd turned someone down for the job."

Katie sighed and gave the floor a last swipe, finally satisfied no possible trace of the grave remained.

"I'm sorry I interrupted whatever you boys were doing. I think I'll be okay up here with my dark archeologist if you want to get back to it."

Ken put his arm around her waist and kissed her cheek.

"You sure? We were just knocking around the old home place, clearing out Granny's old garden patch."

"I'll be fine," Katie said. "My head was deep in lawyer stuff when I almost stepped on Pashmina's latest treasure. You know I'm rotten company at times like that. If fresh veggies are in it for us, go, dig."

For the first time in days, Pashmina didn't linger by the door or try to dart out. Katie found her sound asleep on her cushion in front of the wood stove. The cat didn't twitch a whisker for the rest of the night.

CHAPTER 6

Sheriff Meade turned out to be the kind of law enforcement officer Katie most liked working with on criminal cases. Calm, steady, and unruffled by whatever strange thing might be going on around her. She was Katie's height, too, with gleaming blonde hair caught back in a thick braid down the back of her brown uniform.

She even took notes on her smart phone rather than the tiny flip notebook most officers still seemed to use. Katie liked her immediately.

"I'll ask around," the sheriff said as she, Katie, and Ken walked in a circle around the house. "Have folks up here keep an eye out for muddy tracks or anything else strange. It could be something as simple as a big tree dying during a bad winter. The ground stayed frozen solid until a couple of weeks ago. That makes it heave sometimes. Do you happen to know which direction she runs off to?"

"I have no idea," Katie said. "By the time I chase after her, she's out of sight."

"Well, the tree line's close to the house all around," the sheriff said. "Makes sense. If you do catch her going a certain way, be sure to let me know. Cats can be the devil to keep inside once they get a taste for sneaking by you. We'll see what we can figure out."

Pashmina darted out when Katie took the garbage out that evening, only returning sometime in the middle of the night. The mossy, earthy smell of her fur when she jumped up on the bed sent Katie stumbling through the house, searching for whatever fresh horror her happily purring cat had returned with. Nothing, fresh or dried.

The next morning, what looked like a clump of leathery leaves with long bits of grass attached waited in the middle of the sunroom.

When Katie poked it with the broom and it flopped over, she finally did scream.

What Pashmina brought home turned out to be a bit of scalp and hair.

The macabre offerings continued throughout the week, and Pashmina's determination to get out only grew stronger. Katie found another finger, two toes, and an ear, all wrinkled and dried out.

She and Ken talked to Dave about having an entryway built when they left to try to keep the mighty feline explorer under some kind of control. No one loved the idea of breaking the clean lines of the house that way, but a double set of doors, the closest they could get to a kitty airlock, might actually work.

Neither the sheriff or any of the landowners could track down where the lost bits were coming from, not even on surveyor's maps. Katie started to dread her sunroom and what offering would await.

Her imagination and bad dreams didn't prepare her for what Pashmina did leave next.

At first, she thought her pet had returned to her former

habit of mice. Katie never dreamed she'd be relieved to see a bloody smear on the tile. Her relief didn't last long.

The afternoon sun was dim with the sky heavy and overcast, threatening a late season snow. Katie was nearly upon the mess, scrubbing supplies in hand, before she turned on the light.

"Ken!"

She staggered back, and only the overstuffed chair behind her kept her from falling.

Pashmina jumped down from Katie's reading corner, purring and rubbing against the wall, the couch, everything she walked by.

Katie tried control herself, but she was nearly hyperventilating by the time her husband ran around the corner.

"Katie? What's wrong?"

She could only point with one hand. The other covered her mouth in a desperate attempt to keep her lunch where it belonged.

The bloody thing on the floor wasn't part of a mouse or a squirrel or even a bird.

A fresh human ear joined the long list of horrifying trophies.

"What the *hell*?" Ken fumbled and nearly dropped his phone. "Don't touch anything until Sheriff Meade gets here."

"Don't worry," Katie whispered. She gritted her teeth, but her delirious mind wondering whether the ear was still warm was too much. She barely made it to the bathroom.

By the time she rinsed her mouth out and washed her face, Ken was in the kitchen. He'd locked Pashmina in the bedroom. Katie hated to admit it to herself, but she was relieved.

The idea of the fastidious creature delicately cleaning blood off her fur almost got her stomach started again.

"The sheriff will be here in an hour," Ken said, running his fingers through his hair. "Dave sooner."

"I don't understand this. Sheriff Meade said no one's been buried up here for a long time, didn't she? That looked…" Katie paused for a deep breath. "That looked a lot fresher than even from a funeral home."

"Well yeah. They would have drained…never mind. Get some water or something, Sweetheart. You still look green."

Katie laughed, amazed at such a bizarre response under the circumstances.

"My dear, water simply will not do. I'm making myself a nice, cold gin and tonic. Want one?"

Ken stared at her for a second, then he smiled.

"I'll take you up on that as soon as Sheriff Meade leaves."

Dave showed up around the time Katie finished her drink, but before she could decide whether or not to have a second.

"I'm sure we had a bad connection there," he said, brushing snowflakes from his beard and shoulders. "You didn't say a *fresh* human ear, did you? Tell me you didn't."

"Afraid so," Ken said. "Go have a look for yourself."

Dave returned a few minutes later, shaking his head.

"I'll be damned. You said Sheriff Meade is on her way, too?"

"Should be here any minute," Ken said. "So what would Granny have to say about this one, Dave? You heard a lot more of her tales than I ever did."

Dave raised his thick black eyebrows, the corners of his mouth turning down.

"This one might be beyond even her wisdom. I don't think any of Granny's cats ever brought back anything quite like this. Or if they did, she didn't tell me."

"The wicked bone," Katie said under her breath.

"What was that?" Ken reached for her hand. "I couldn't hear you."

"Dave told me about your grandmother saying everything and everyone had a wicked bone. The parts the cats won't eat."

Ken nodded, but now he looked worried.

"Right," Dave said. "Everything except her dogs."

"Except her dogs," Katie echoed. Her head felt swimmy and her skin too hot, but not from the gin. "Maybe this is the part of whoever that was. The part the cat won't eat."

"I don't understand," Ken said. "You're not making sense, Katie."

"You think I don't know that?" Katie smiled to soften the words. "Come with me. I want to get a closer look at…it."

Ken started to argue, but she touched his lips with her fingertips.

"I'm serious, and I'm not drunk. Come on."

Both men followed her, and Katie was sure they glanced at each other behind her back. For once she didn't care. Something had hold of her mind, her Lawyer Mind she called it. She'd learned a long time ago to pay attention when that happened.

She didn't let go of Ken's hand, though.

"Do you have your phone?" she said, standing a few inches away from the blood. "Either of you?"

"You want pictures?" Dave said.

"Not pictures. The flashlight."

Dave shrugged, pulled out his phone, and thumbed the light on. Katie leaned as close as she dared, not wanting to breathe in the metallic scent. Curious as she was, that would set off her jumpy stomach again for sure.

"What is that?" Ken let go of her hand and squatted, both of his knees crackling like gunshots. "Something glinting."

"We shouldn't touch anything," Dave said, stepping forward himself. "Not until the sheriff gets here."

"I see it too," Katie said.

She leaned closer, her hand on Ken's shoulder.

There, on the red-streaked earlobe.

Three tiny blue stones.

Katie's head floated again, and she clutched at Ken to keep from staggering into the mess.

"Dave," she said, "did you ever ask that guy about the graveyards? The tractor guy?"

He looked confused for a second.

"You mean Jay Bishop? No, I didn't get a chance to. Not really. I left him a voice message last week. Haven't seen him or heard back."

"He had an earring like that." Katie pointed at the ear. "Just like it."

"You don't think…" Ken said.

"Which way did he live?" Katie said. "Which way from here? Do you know where his house was?"

The rolling queasiness in her belly gave way to a cold, solid certainty. Katie couldn't explain it, even to herself.

But she *knew*.

"He…hang on." Dave rubbed at the bridge of his nose, the same way Ken did when his was confused and trying to pull it together. "He said he'd moved into the old Blevins place, but that was months ago. West. It's to the west."

"Then let's go see," Katie said. "Before the snow gets too heavy."

The two men followed her only a few seconds behind, and she was thankful they didn't argue first. Her Lawyer Mind insisted she was still on the right track, while her regular mind and the rest of her insisted she was crazy.

They walked less than a hundred feet to the west through huge snowflakes floating in slow motion. The ground wasn't covered yet, but it would be before the sun went down.

At the edge of the woods, the grass gave way to leaves and brushy undergrowth.

And a massive, flattened spot in the brush, turning each flake scarlet as soon as they touched the ground.

"Katie, what…" Ken said, staring at the ground. "How did you know to look here?"

"I didn't. But Sheriff Meade said to see if we could catch which way Pashmina ran off."

"Pashmina didn't make anything that big," Dave said.

"Something did." Katie pointed to flattened spots leading away from the blood, heading onto the grass and toward the house. The snow was filling them in already, but the shape was unmistakable.

Giant paw prints.

Like a panther's.

"That's too big to be a bobcat," Dave said, his voice barely above a whisper. He started to kneel and ended up on his knees instead. He held his hand over one of the tracks, barely covering it. "Or any kind of dog."

"What did your Granny say when she sent her cats out?" Katie said. "Go out and earn your keep, and something else?"

Dave looked up at her, eyes wide and face pale.

"Come back a cat. She said best come back a cat."

Ken shook his head and crossed his arms.

"What, you're saying a panther did this? Something to do with Granny's tall tales?"

"I don't know," Katie said. "But where did the tracks go?"

All three of them stepped backward, staring down at the rapidly disappearing grass. The huge footprints were still visible heading right toward the house. Toward the sunroom door they'd been leaving open when Pashmina darted outside.

The tracks stopped about ten feet away from the woods.

"We have to tell Sheriff Meade," Ken said, still shaking his head. "None of this makes any sense."

"It doesn't make sense to me, either," Katie said. "But as your attorney, I'd advise you to think about how this looks first. A severed ear in our sunroom, and a big blood puddle right beside the house?"

"What are we supposed to do, then?" Ken snapped. "Pretend we didn't see any of this?"

"Hang on." Dave grabbed Ken's shoulder. "I'm not saying I think… I'm not saying *what* I think because I can't. But maybe the sheriff should check the place out. Where Jay was staying, I mean. She'd need to go there anyway, right?"

"How long til the snow covers this up?" Katie said. "The blood, the tracks?"

"Just a few minutes at this rate." Ken rubbed his eyes, then glanced at the blood again. It was already turning pink, well on its way to white. "I can't believe I'm even considering this."

Katie snorted, trying not to laugh out loud.

"After Pashmina has been bringing body parts into the house for days? What I'd consider has adjusted itself considerably. Let's get back inside. We won't even know what we're suggesting until someone finds this Jay person. Or gets a look at his house."

CHAPTER 7

THE HOUSE WAS the key to everything.

Sheriff Meade showed up less than half an hour later in her official brown version of Ken's Jeep, with two deputies riding along. Katie tried not to let her relief show when one of them recognized the blue earring before she had to point it out. They headed right out to look for Jay Bishop.

By the time they returned, pale and quiet, the snow had wiped out all evidence of blood and huge paw prints beside Ken and Katie's house.

None of that mattered after what the officers found over at the old Blevins place.

Sheriff Meade and the two young men with her sat around Katie's kitchen, cooling mugs of coffee gripped in their hands.

"The door was open," the sheriff said. "There was blood there and out into the yard. Not a trace of anything else, though. No bodies."

"He'd seen plenty of bodies at some point," one of the deputies said, his voice trembling.

Sheriff Meade nodded.

"That Blevins place never was much more than a single-room cabin, but he had it stuffed full. Boxes full of old jewelry, gold teeth, wire-frame glasses. Still musty and stinking of the bodies they were buried with. None of it worth a lot by itself, though some of the diamonds and such would have added up. But enough to get your attention. Looked to me like he was packing up to leave. We would have heard if something like this happened at the big cemeteries in town."

"Something like what?" Ken said. He held his own mug, and Katie was sure she'd seen him pour a shot of whiskey in.

"I suspect he'd been digging up the old family graveyards," Sheriff Meade said. "That would explain the things your cat brought home, too. That little backhoe he had was light enough to make it up the trails, especially when the ground was frozen. I expect we'll find he wasn't as careful putting things back together when he was finished."

"A grave robber," Dave said. "In this day and age."

"Still don't know where the ear came from," the sheriff said. "Or where the rest of him went. But we'll keep looking."

"I hope he's gone for good," Katie said, getting to her feet. "Excuse me for a second?"

When she opened the bedroom door, Pashmina wasn't curled up on Katie's pillow sleeping, the way she usually did when she was alone. The silken black cat waited just inside the door, tail curled around her feet.

She blinked up at Katie, long and slow.

Ken always said they had to praise Pashmina for a successful hunt.

"What have you been doing, gorgeous?" Katie picked up the intelligent, wondrous creature. "Taking care of the

86

problem yourself when the humans were too silly to catch all the hints you left for us?"

Pashmina only purred, settling herself onto Katie's shoulder.

She kneaded with one tiny foot, then the other, over and over again.

KARI KILGORE

AUTHOR OF THE WORRY TRAP AND WICKED BONE

In Service to a Superior Species

For everyone who offered a helping hand
during a year when we all needed one

CHAPTER 1

JANET HAD ALWAYS liked animals *much* more than she liked people.

So the chance to pretty much shelter in place as the Emergency Feline Domestic Servant for the university animal hospital during the pandemic of 2020 was a dream come true.

At first.

Even a few weeks in, the outbreak could still seem distant, far away, at least to anyone who wasn't paying attention.

The collection of graceful brick buildings and curving sidewalks nestled into a beautiful valley deep in the Appalachian Mountains, with the first flush of spring pink buds breaking across the trees.

The setting felt isolated, safe. Secure and cozy. Downright calm and peaceful compared to the scramble for hand sanitizer and toilet paper out in the world, and the scramble for hospital beds and ventilators to come.

And the campus was beautiful, too. Several years' worth of horticulture students had planted a dizzying array of early spring bulbs, helped out by carpentry and bricklaying apprentices building beds in every imaginable shape and size.

Masses of cup-shaped crocuses in blue, yellow, and white, their blooms smaller than a golf ball. Bunches of sweet-smelling hyacinths, the grape variety like tiny purple pyramids, the standard more like cylinders of white and pink and blue and purple.

Waves of cheery yellow daffodils and a breathtaking array of irises were only a couple of weeks away, not to mention cherry blossoms and lilacs lining the walkways.

Janet enjoyed the floral show as always on her solitary daily walks. Maybe even more than usual, since the air was remarkably clear of the remains of gas and coal, and the only sound was the cool breeze and her own footsteps.

But even considering her normal reclusive ways, her heart ached at the flowers reaching their colorful peak on a campus empty of students, professors, staff, and pretty much everyone else.

She normally lived in a sweet little one-story brick house a few minutes away, but her new temporary digs adjacent to the animal hospital were nicer than she expected. A few years ago, an extremely generous donor had left an equally generous endowment—with one unusual condition.

All the money was earmarked to provide housing for people with beloved pets undergoing treatment.

Early discussions about the possible campus closure emphasized provisions for the handful of animals who couldn't go home for whatever reason, and who was going to take care of them.

Janet volunteered for observation duty in the dedicated cat boarding and treatment facility right away. Time without people, and *with* books, movies, and music, and above all, cats, sounded heavenly to her introverted and sometimes shy self.

And the idea of keeping herself separate from what looked more and more like a serious disease was exactly what her jangled nerves needed. A rotten case of the flu a couple of years ago that led to a bout with pneumonia was never far from her mind these days.

She struggled with the desire to go inward and stay away from news altogether versus the need to constantly be online reading and learning as much as she possibly could about what was going on.

Furry cuddles took her mind off her worries like magic, especially with several cats to tend to all at once.

So by the time the difficult decision to close down the campus was made, she and her long-haired gray tabby boy Bitu were already settled into a one-bedroom apartment nicer than any of the local hotels (who all also accepted pets). Bitu often accompanied Janet for her shift at the hospital.

Just as well, because he was more of a people person than she'd ever be.

He walked in front of her as usual on her morning stroll through stark white corridors toward what she liked to call the Feline Residential Hall, huge fluffy gray tail aloft, the tip gently tilting back and forth.

He didn't mind being let out of his carrier and walking himself one little bit, thank you very much.

Janet still marveled at what a gorgeous cat he'd turned into after his rough start at a coal mine of all places.

He'd been a plump and well-fed kitten, with all the mice he could catch, and soft-hearted coal miners making sure he had plenty of scraps and treats. But before Bitu was a year old, one of them brought him in because he'd pulled a bunch of his hair out. Turned out once warm weather brought the return of flea season, the poor kitty's raging flea allergy flared up something awful, leaving him an itchy, scraggly mess.

Now he was a fifteen-pound fluff ball, with adorable

tabby markings of a broad M on his forehead and backwards Fs on his cheeks, and well-defined racing stripes everywhere else. His long black and gray hair gleamed and flounced when he ran.

He took his Resident Greeter duties quite seriously, too.

The Feline Residential Hall (more commonly known as the boarding room) was as soothing and quiet as the canine version on the other side of the hospital could be raucous and loud. The overhead lights were dim, the air warm. Three rows of steel cages lined the walls of the small room, each wider than a normal kennel space for a cat.

Only seven of the twenty-four cages were occupied at the moment, each of them in the waist-high row. And each of those cages looked more like a very posh apartment that many humans would enjoy spending time in.

The animal hospital had its own supplies of blankets and towels and cushions, often donated by grateful pet guardians. Nice as those were, none of these special cats had to rely on the house supplies. Thick, soft cushions, a dizzying array of toys, and in more than one case, photos and even clothing of the humans owned by these cats decorated their temporary abodes.

Janet would spend a good part of her day in the Playground—a cat wonderland of a room stuffed full of climbing, scratching, tunneling, windows, and everything else a boarding or rehabilitating feline could desire. Sending photos and videos of each individual cat's playtime, coordinating FaceTime visits, and exchanging text message or calls to reassure the lonely humans that the cats were somehow doing perfectly fine in their absence.

These pampered critters didn't even have to tolerate their sanitary facilities in their living space. At the back of each cage, a black rubber cat door led out to a small litter box area. Janet would scoop and refresh each one as soon as breakfast was over, working in what she termed the Servant's Passage—the hallway behind this main room.

No matter how many times she saw it happen, she still smiled as more cats than not dashed out to their privy to immediately dirty up their newly clean boxes. Bitu would be among them, using the box she had set up for him in one of the bottom cages.

Right now, Bitu stopped in front of each kitty apartment, lifting his head and letting out a long, curious *meaaaaaow* as Janet slipped her fingers through the silvery bars for her own greeting. This was mostly a sociable bunch, as if they knew they might be here for a while. Thankfully none of them were sick, either.

Almost all of the cats chirped or burbled or meowed their replies to Bitu first.

Greeting the superior species, of course.

They then stood on their gorgeous cushions—chosen to coordinate with their coat color, obviously—and stretched with their backs arched and their tails reaching toward their heads. Finally they delicately stepped toward the front of the cage to accept Janet's caresses.

Much head-butting and mouth-rubbing of her fingers ensued, by calico and tortie and tuxedo, striped and spotted and solid, orange and gray and black. Janet's constant hand-washing apparently convinced the cats they needed to claim her as their own again and again.

Some of the pets here and over on the dog side had people terribly busy at the nearby university hospital, and afraid they wouldn't be able to spend enough time with their pets. A couple had people recently returned from overseas, relieved to have their cherished companions well cared for while they were in quarantine in a distant city.

And one poor sweet kitty named Moxie owned a person

who was terribly ill with the new virus over at the hospital, and she seemed to know it.

After stopping to send up his perky greeting to each of the relatively happy cats, Bitu stopped in front of Moxie's home away from home. Rather than raising his head and calling out his version of "Good *morning*," he sat, wrapping his tail around his feet.

He purred softly, watching the bars the whole time.

Janet walked over just as quietly, peering inside instead of reaching for the bars right away. Moxie had scooted her bright pink cushion as far away from the front as she could get it, nearly blocking the door to the litter box area. She'd piled a purple fuzzy blanket up on one edge like a tiny barricade, so only a hint of sleek, pure black showed.

After a few seconds, Moxie raised her head. One orange eye opened, then the other. She slow-blinked at Janet, lifted her slender tail in a dainty greeting, and snuggled down behind the blanket again.

Bitu got up and rubbed the length of his body against Janet's ankle, then circled around to rub the other. As if to remind her that while he was worried about Moxie (and her human), he wanted to make sure Janet remembered how lucky she was to be with him.

"You're right, as always," she said, leaning down to pick him up. He put his front paws on her shoulder, leaned his soft face against her neck, and purred even louder. "I *am* lucky to be with you. Now let's get everyone's breakfast ready so we can have ours, too."

CHAPTER 2

JANET KNEW THE ANXIOUS, scary outside world had intruded on her peaceful cat-filled week when she got the text message.

Her phone buzzed in her pocket just as she filled the last bowl full of cat guardian-supplied kibble. The row of eight small steel bowls reflected off the matching table, full of whatever each of their honored guests was used to eating at home. More kibble in different shapes and sizes, canned food, or a mix of both filled the tiny supply room with aroma she couldn't exactly call *pleasant*.

But the familiarity of years spent living with or caring for cats brought its own comfort.

She'd have her own Grape Nuts and soy milk and blueberries and mug full of strong Earl Gray tea soon enough, with a little table and chair she wheeled into the Feline Residential Hall so she and the cats could enjoy their breakfasts together.

The supply room was brighter and cooler than the kitty condo room next door, with shelves lining the walls in the same positions as the kennels. The occupied shelves were stuffed full of extra blankets, toys, and treats, so much so that the supply of food in each could be a challenge to wedge back inside.

Janet pulled her phone out as she replaced the last bag of cat food. When she thumbed open the message from the university hospital director a second later, she was distantly grateful through cold chills that she'd waited to read it. Otherwise she probably would have dropped the bag and had to clean up a thousand brown bits of food rolling around the black rubberized tiles.

She shook her head, then leaned against the table to read the message over again. Bitu jumped up on the table, but he ignored food entirely for the first time since Janet first met him.

Instead he butted his head against her arm repeatedly until she ran a trembling hand along his back. He demonstrated a perfect cat elevator-butt response by lifting his backside and tail with every stroke.

The number of confirmed cases in their tiny university town had jumped from eight to thirty-three overnight. She knew the state had expanded testing over the past few days, much of it right here at the university.

But the increase took her breath anyway.

Out of that number, enough were seriously ill that no less than eleven more cats and seven more dogs would be joining the boarders by...later that afternoon?

She blew out a breath through pursed lips, causing Bitu to blink and lay his ears to the side.

"Sorry sweetheart. Looks like we're about to have a *whole* lot of company."

She tapped the message to call Shannon Mullins, the hospital director. This was too big for a bunch of back-and-forth texts and escalating potential for misunderstanding. The call connected before the second ring.

"Hey Janet," Shannon said, and Janet could hear how exhausted she was in those two words. "Really sorry to dump all this on you. All the local boarding facilities and veterinarians are full up or on short staff. And to be perfectly honest, the folks getting treatment who've had their animals boarded here in the past have asked to have their critters nearby."

"I understand. You know I'll do the best I can for them. Bitu will too. And I'm sorry to dump this on *you*, but I'm going to need… Well, eighteen cats is going to be tough."

Shannon let out a sigh loud enough for Janet to hear.

"Yeah, that makes sense. Of course, you can't handle that on your own. Neither can the woman on the dog side. Let me put you on hold and send a couple of messages…"

Janet walked in several slow circles around the steel table. Bitu walked right along beside her on the shiny surface, alternately head-butting her hand and speeding up so she rubbed his back, then circling around to start the whole thing over again.

And hard to imagine as it might have been just a couple of minutes ago, he *still* ignored the food. Bitu walking by food, especially the incredibly stinky wet food he never got to eat at home, would normally be as likely as him standing up on his back feet, asking for the car keys, and heading into town to buy himself a case of tuna.

Of course the situation in their town and state and country and the whole *world* was unimaginable a few shorts weeks ago.

"Okay," Shannon said, startling Janet. "This will turn everything into a whole different kind of situation for you, but I've got a couple of people who can come in to help. Both live close by, no one else at home so they can stay in the apartments there with you. They work here in the classroom side of the hospital normally, so they've been home since we closed campus."

Bitu walked by Janet's arm again, rubbing against her as he slid the front part of his body down onto the table. His backside was still up, though, and his amazingly fluffy gray and black tail waved in the air like a flag. Janet hadn't realized she'd stopped walking until then.

She didn't want to admit to the jolt of anxiety at the idea of people she didn't know at all working in such close quarters with her, for who knew how long.

Not to mention the fear of possibly getting sick herself rather than riding it out in quiet solitude.

"So we'll need to do the whole protocol with masks and everything," she said. "We have extra food on the way for the cats? And litter?"

"We've got that covered. The masks and things, I mean, and we'll of course run rapid tests on all three of you today. The owners are helping with the rest. Some of the local college kids are running an online campaign, too. Asking for donations for the cats and dogs and whatever other animals we have tucked away. It's going really well, been on TV and radio and everything."

She took a breath and paused for a second, and Janet wondered if Shannon was tearing up as much as she was.

Those poor kids.

Their education stopped cold, or at least playing out in a new and distant format, and they were busy thinking of animals who weren't even their own.

"They're even asking for food for you *human* types," Shannon went on. "Believe it or not. Money for ebooks and movie downloads, too. They might even score some of that most precious of substances known to humanity at the moment, *toilet paper*. Though I gotta say it would probably be easier if you all just learn to squat and use the litter boxes instead."

Janet snorted out laughter before she could stop herself,

and Bitu whipped around to look at her so fast his fluffy coat flared around him. He blinked once, then sneezed.

"Well okay then. That settles it. I'll get everyone's breakfast served and clean up after them so we'll be ready for the new arrivals. We'll make sure to set aside three extra-deep litter boxes for potential human use while we're at it."

Shannon laughed too, relief clear in her voice. Bitu walked in a circle around Janet's hand, twining his tail around her wrist, then stood with his front feet against her chest.

She leaned down so he could boop his pink nose against hers, the cool touch reassuring and calming her as always.

"Thank you so much, Janet. I know I'm asking a lot."

"You're welcome. I know you're *doing* a lot. Are you okay over there? Everyone holding up?"

Shannon sighed again, louder and longer than before.

"We're managing. It's rough, I won't lie about that. But we'll get through, especially with good people like you and these local kids doing everything they can to make it easier."

Bitu rubbed his chin against Janet's, his purr loud enough that she felt it in her own chest.

Along with a slight loosening of her knots of fear and worry.

"Good," she said. "Take care of yourself, Shannon. I do have a question though, about these people coming in. I'm glad they work at the hospital, even on the classroom side. Truly I am. But are they *cat* people? Not everyone is cut out for isolation with this many creatures who require attendance like tiny little gods."

Shannon laughed under her breath. "Absolutely. They're each bringing a cat of their own, in fact. They're fine with keeping their shy kitties in their apartments, so no worries about cramping Bitu's style. They're both going a little stir-crazy, to be honest, and jumped at the chance to do something. I'll round up a couple of dog people to help out on the other side next."

Janet smiled down at Bitu and returned his loving slow blink. She scooped him up and held him close, rubbing his head with her cheek.

"Don't worry, Bitu," she whispered. "They're cat people."

When she gently set him down on the table, he went straight to his food and dug in.

Apparently she'd said the magic words.

"We'll be ready," she said into the phone. "Just let me know what time they'll get here and what I need to do. Oh, and Shannon? I know you're slammed there, but could you possibly check on someone for me? He was one of the first patients brought in. I have his sweet kitty Moxie here. She's worried enough about him that I'm worried about her."

"Yes, Mr. Sullivan, right? I'll get an update and get back to you right away."

CHAPTER 3

Janet was just swallowing her last sip of bergamot-scented tea when her phone buzzed in her pocket again.

The Feline Residence Hall had fallen quiet after the storm of crunches and chewing and pauses for a drink of water, followed by the tap and swoosh as the cat doors allowed pampered diners to dash out to relieve themselves.

Now the only sound was the occasional licking noise of the communal post-meal grooming hour.

She had no doubt at least half of them would hold back enough to head right back out to pay a bonus litter box visit as soon as she cleaned up their post-breakfast offerings.

Bitu had already managed his business in his bottom-row run and curled himself up in Janet's lap for a good wash and purr. She reached for her phone carefully so she wouldn't disturb his tiny black-and-gray-striped majesty.

"Hey Janet," Shannon said, sounding much less weary than before. "Got someone here who really wants to speak to someone there. I think he'd prefer to talk face-to-face if he can."

Janet gasped, warmth and tears welling up from her chest.

"Mr. Sullivan?"

"Sure is. Turns out he came off the ventilator earlier this morning. The very first words he managed to whisper were along the lines of 'How's my Moxie?'"

"Oh, that's *wonderful!* Hang on, she's right here."

Janet kissed Bitu right in the middle of the M on his forehead, then gently set him on the floor. She got up and walked over to Moxie's cage and blinked back more tears.

For the first time since she arrived—the same day Mr. Sullivan had—Moxie walked back and forth, rubbing right up against the front of her cage. Her gleaming black hair rippled as she pressed against the bars, and she chittered to herself almost as if she'd spotted a bird.

Janet pushed the button to switch to video and saw a close-up of Shannon's face. Well, she saw a close-up of a plastic face shield with a mask underneath, really, but the big grin was still visible underneath.

Janet grinned in return.

"I've got someone here who's about to burst from wanting to talk to her special person."

The view shifted, and she saw a man with dark skin, his stubbly cheeks and eyes looking a bit sunken. A clear plastic tube ran from his ears to his nose, and even on the phone's screen, Janet could tell he was exhausted.

But his eyes were bright and his smile even brighter.

"You have my Moxie there, Miss Janet?" he whispered.

"I sure do, Mr. Sullivan. I'm so glad you're doing better, but not half as glad as she is."

She turned the phone around, and Moxie stopped pacing at once, her huge orange eyes locked onto the screen. Her purr started up right away, and Janet heard her somehow managing to meow at the same time over her beloved person's soft whispers.

Bitu twined around her ankles, then jumped up onto her breakfast table. Ignoring the dregs of soy milk in the bowl for the first time in his life with her, he stared at her as intently as Moxie stared at Mr. Sullivan.

Janet scooped him up again without moving the phone and held him close to her ear, listening to his own purring rumble.

"Everything is changing, my sweet Bitu. All around us, and maybe some of it is going to change forever. But as long as we take care of each other, we're going to be okay."

KARI KILGORE

AUTHOR OF ODDS AND ENDINGS AND INTENTIONS

The Magic Cat
of the Hidden Springs
Inn and Spa

For Zortea

Who seems to be put together out of spare parts
but her heart works better than most people's do

CHAPTER 1

As FAR AS Henry Satterfield was concerned, the owners of the Hidden Springs Inn and Spa had clearly found the line when it came to tasteful holiday decorations. And then promptly jumped over that line and kept running, in matching pairs of red and green bedazzled high heeled boots.

Five fully decorated Christmas trees dominated the broad lobby, each highlighting a different style that did not coordinate with the others. The biggest was a perfectly shaped Fraser Fir, with the stiff, stubby leaves loaded down with every variety of non-traditional ornament available. Dark, modern colors, LED lights that oozed from one color to the next, not a scrap of tinsel to be seen. At least that one smelled good, fresh and green.

Surrounding that were what Henry thought of as the Especially Smelly Ghosts of Christmas Past, from a Nineties department store special that came pre-decorated, a fake bendy limbed Seventies version reeking of cigarettes, all the way back to an honest-to-goodness aluminum model that reeked of other things, each loaded with decade-appropriate ornaments and potentially hazardous lighting.

The only tree Henry secretly loved was the one the inn's current owners—Suzie and Lloyd Fletcher—had given him complete freedom with. The Fletchers had asked him to pick and decorate something none of the other inns and hotels in the quaint little tourist town would have.

Henry had done a spectacular job with that one, and he wasn't the only one to say so. A brand new, extremely trendy and gorgeous solid black tree, tall and narrow, in a corner by itself. Intense violet, indigo, and blood-red lights sparkled against silver ornaments of every shape and size. Guests and Hidden Springs residents alike were drawn to that tree like goth moths to an inky black flame the second they walked through the jingle bell-laden door.

Another adjustment Henry had talked the Fletchers to making over the five years he'd worked school vacations here was adding other traditions. Besides his delightfully dark tree (which would pull double-duty at Halloween), the room held traditional and modern menorahs for Jewish guests alongside Kwanzaa displays with red, green, and black candles. Groovy old peace signs and doves dug out from the same basement storage crate as the aluminum tree competed with repurposed disco balls from a decade later.

He'd even managed to turn up the old pagan traditions with extra holly, acorns, and oak leaves to go with the dizzying array of crosses and stars and praying angels.

Of course when the Fletchers added in enough glitter and snowflakes and Santas to stock a department store, no one was likely to get bent out of shape over one religious tradition or another.

Lloyd Fletcher came bustling through just then, humming a perfectly in-tune version of *Deck the Halls* just as loud as his voice would go. Still, it was a bit jarring against the slow and ponderous choir version of *O Little Town of*

Bethlehem playing over the stereo. Henry gratefully took the excuse to turn the "music" off.

Lloyd was almost a foot shorter than Henry's lanky six-foot-two, and just about as round and jolly as the Santa-man himself. All the lobby's overly cheery lights and sparkles gleamed off of his head, and a holiday-induced grin decorated his round face. Henry figured he looked downright gloomy in comparison, with his short brown hair and goatee emphasizing his own longish face.

"Are you *sure* you don't mind staying, Henry?" he said for at least the twentieth time in the last hour. "Your folks are only a couple of hours away. Plenty of time to get there before that special order Christmas Eve snowstorm rolls in."

"I volunteered, Mr. Fletcher. Remember? I could use the extra cash and the quiet time to catch up on my reading. My brain needs a break from math and engineering. Especially if I get to chow down on those cookies."

Mr. Fletcher looked down and actually drew back, apparently surprised he was carrying a holly-shaped plate full of fresh chocolate chip, peanut butter, and sparkly pastel sugar cookies.

"Well, maybe not *all* of them," Mr. Fletcher said. "Someone might stop by yet."

He tucked the plate among the piles of oranges, tangerines, apples, and nuts already displayed on the tall check-in desk. There was enough room for any surprise guests to sign in on the electronic tablet, but only just. A smaller table off to the side held coffee, hot water for tea, and a big copper pot full of fragrant spiced apple cider steaming away over a hot plate.

"I think we've got enough out here to feed Santa and all the elves," Henry said. "Mrs. Fletcher already told me to bring the fudge out once it cools. And that she left enough food in the kitchen to feed me and the hundred guests who won't be showing up on Christmas Eve in a snowstorm."

Mr. Fletcher grasped his hands together under his chin.

"Oooooh, she made that New England fudge, didn't she? The brown sugar kind. I never can remember what it's called."

"She did, and she reminded me to tell you to keep your hands off. She's got some packed up in the car and ready to go. Speaking of go…"

This time Mr. Fletcher jumped as if one of Santa's elves had goosed him a good one. He glanced wide-eyed at his wrist watch.

"Suzie's gonna kill me. If you're sure, I'll get going then." He raised his voice and called over his shoulder. "Ms. Zee! Come out here and say goodnight!"

A jingle sounded from upstairs, then came pounding down like a herd of miniature elephants wearing bells on their collars. A nine-pound gray tabby cat with a crooked tail, tiny head, short legs, and long body shouldn't make that much noise. But Zortea, the official Hidden Springs Inn and Spa Greeter and Rodent Control Squad, managed every time.

Zortea thundered into view with a musical burble, irregular tail so high it lay nearly flat along her back. She twisted around Mr. Fletcher's legs until he picked her up. The cheerful burble instantly turned into an extremely silly and non-threatening humming growl.

"I know you don't like it when we pick you up, Fussybritches," Mr. Fletcher cooed, holding the offended feline against his chest. "I just had to say *Meowy* Christmas, Zortea. Ting-zilla. Zang-teeah."

Henry had been around dogs and cats his entire life, and he knew how many goofy nicknames they could accumulate. But he'd never heard anything like the ever-growing collection people seemed driven to bestow upon Zortea.

"The cats at this inn are magic, you know," Mr. Fletcher said, smiling at Henry. "Suzie and I aren't the only ones who met and fell in love right here in this lobby over the years."

The last thing Henry needed tonight was more advice about his rickety love life. That was one of the best reasons for avoiding his perpetually honeymooning parents, not to mention all of his happily married siblings and cousins.

"I always heard it was ghosts, Mr. Fletcher."

"Well, maybe the cats can *see* ghosts. Either way, it's the truth. You take care of Henry now, Tiffle-zee." Mr. Fletcher deposited Zortea on the rug depicting Santa's sleigh and all nine reindeer, then stepped behind the desk to give Henry a quick hug. "I know you want your peace and quiet, but I hope someone does stop in and stay for the night. I worry about you getting lonely."

Henry smiled and waved toward the door.

"I'll be perfectly fine here with Zortea the magic cat. Go! You're going to get me in trouble with your missus!"

One more hug, and Mr. Fletcher was gone.

Henry sighed as he reached down to rub the cat's back. She immediately resumed singing to herself. He got up, got himself a mug of spiced cider and one of each kind of cookie, and settled onto the snowflake-patterned couch with his e-reader. After a few somewhat painful circles, Zortea settled down onto his shoulder and started purring.

He changed the playlist from A Special Brand of Traditional Holiday Torture to a list of his own: Holiday Songs He Could Actually Tolerate. He smiled at Vince Guaraldi's mellow *A Charlie Brown Christmas* floating through the air, as light and fantastic as the snow he could see starting outside the window.

He hoped anyone who did get caught in the storm would

stop at one of the big chain hotels on the interstate rather than making their way to the inn.

A little bit lonely for Christmas Eve?

Sure.

But a thousand and one times better than his parents down in Asheville, and their overstuffed, overheated, and overly full of noisy people holiday crowd.

"You and me, Jingle-zee. You and me."

CHAPTER 2

Steve Lake swore under his breath as the time of arrival on the GPS crept up another ten minutes. At this rate, the last fifty miles of the drive were going to take longer than the first three-hundred-fifty.

A featureless white landscape stretched in all directions, unmarked by minor inconveniences like the shape of the interstate highway he was trying to travel. His sedan's wiper blades did their best, but they simply weren't designed to shove huge wedges of snow away over and over again. The fact that just as much snow covered the windshield on every return trip of the wipers didn't improve matters.

The car was warm enough, thank goodness, but the defrost set on high was drying Steve's contacts out until they felt like jagged little shards of eyeball glass. He forced his hands to relax on the wheel and rotated his shoulders.

He wasn't sure if the smell of overcooked gas station coffee on his breath or the nervous sweat rising up from his armpits was worse. His growling stomach would have greatly preferred to have something else for comparison. Especially if that something was unhealthy and absolutely delicious stress-relief food. His mom's spicy macaroni and cheese, maybe, or his father's fresh-baked gooey cinnamon rolls.

A few tractor trailers joined him on this insane voyage through snow globe hell. He could barely make out one a ways in front of him by the high taillights. Another behind him kept getting closer, but Steve was afraid to speed up much.

His wheels kind of fit in the deep ruts left by the truck ahead. Sort of. The sedan slid from side to side way too much for his comfort.

He'd turned the stereo off a few slow, anxious miles back so he could concentrate. But now his ears were begging for anything to break up the low, crunching hum of his tires and the slushy whoosh of the wipers.

Weren't there *any* exits down here at the tail end of Virginia? He would have sworn he hadn't seen one for at least a hundred miles, but that couldn't be right. He'd made this drive dozens of times over the last five years since he'd moved from East Tennessee to Washington, DC.

His current blazing speed of twenty-three miles an hour might explain the problem.

He'd so wanted to be home with his family tonight, and he'd expected to be more than an hour ago. Besides missing them more than usual since he hadn't been able to make the trip for Thanksgiving, Steve needed a good dose of home-cooked comfort. A rotten breakup in the middle of November hadn't exactly gotten his holiday season off to a spectacular start.

A flash of green to his right, too big to be one of the crawling mileage markers, made Steve's heart jump into his throat.

Could it be?

Might it be?

Yes! An exit!

He hadn't paid any attention to the small towns through here on his drives before, since he was so close to home. But all of a sudden, the unknowns of Hidden Springs, Virginia, sounded like paradise right here off the interstate.

Steve put on his turn signal and slowed even more, watching for a ridge of snow built up in his path. He'd driven in more than enough snowstorms to understand the general procedure. But this monster had taken him by surprise when he was already tired from the trip and ready to be home.

Rain in Washington and rain in Johnson City, Tennessee, the forecast had said. And that was probably true.

The higher elevation through the mountains had other ideas on this Christmas Eve.

For once, Steve was glad the snowplows didn't seem to have made an appearance yet. The snow was thick on the off-ramp, but he didn't have to crash through a plow-moat. The tire noise dropped to a whisper, draining a whole lot of the stress out of his neck and shoulders.

He could still skid into a tree or off one of the unfamiliar small-town roads. But he wouldn't have several tons of semi bearing down on top of him.

He followed the gentle curve, trying to watch the suggestion of a road and read the snow-speckled blue signs at the same time. The first listed gas stations. Full tank of gas, so no. Food? No decent restaurant would be open in this mess on Christmas Eve. Pass.

Accommodations! Two big chain hotels, both probably booked solid in this storm. Steve squinted, trying to catch the text on a third logo that promised it was only 0.3 miles away.

The Hidden Springs Inn and Spa, complete with a cartoon image of steaming hot water. Steve groaned and closed his eyes for a quick second.

He didn't care one bit whether that meant a commercial

hot tub, a hotel bathtub, or an actual hot spring. He wouldn't mind if the inn cost ten times what any of the chains did.

He couldn't think of anything he'd rather do than soak this rotten drive away. He'd call his parents and break the bad news once he was able to pry his fingers loose from the steering wheel.

They wanted him home as badly as he wanted to be there, but he knew they'd understand.

Steve simply couldn't face one more mile in a freak blizzard tonight.

"Please, oh please, kind sir. Tell me you have room at your inn for one more wandering soul tonight."

CHAPTER 3

HENRY JUMPED like he was the one goosed by a mischievous little elf when Zortea leapt from his shoulder to his thigh with no warning. She continued onto the floor with a cheery chirp and jingle, reminding him he'd need to take that bell off so she could go hunting tonight.

Two hours? He tapped the surface of his watch, certain his e-reader had lost track of the time as badly as he had.

Nope, it was indeed eight in the evening. Christmas Evening, to be exact. He'd gotten so far into his seasonally appropriate zombie apocalypse novel that he'd forgotten where he was, and why.

Now Zortea stood on the reindeer rug with her head tilted, almost like a tiny little striped dog. She chirped, going from low to high exactly like a person asking a question, then went galloping toward the front door.

A glance out the window to Henry's left showed at least eight inches of snow had piled up while he was lost in a much more exciting, though inconvenient, world.

"I think you're mistaken, Jangle-zee. No one's out on a night like this. No one sane, anyway."

Henry grunted and grabbed at his pounding heart when bells in all sizes and tones sang out as the front door opened.

A man stepped into the lobby, accompanied by a rush of cold air and a whirling fog of gigantic snowflakes.

"Have I died and gone to holiday heaven?" he said. "Is that Bing Crosby and David *Bowie*?"

Henry took a second to focus back on the real world. Sure enough, *Little Drummer Boy* was rum-pum-pumming away.

"It, um, it sure is. Can I help you?"

The man brushed snow from curly blond hair and a reddish beard before turning his attention to broad shoulders covered with green and black flannel. His smile almost outshone the lights in the aluminum tree.

"I certainly hope so. Are you going to tell me this lovely establishment is not only open, but has a vacancy? And maybe even something hot to eat?"

"Well, yeah. All that, a magic cat, and a hot spring spa. I'm guessing you need a room for the night?"

"In the worst possible way. Wow, The Waitresses, too? And that black tree is the best thing I've seen all day. I love this place already."

Henry got to his feet, grinning at the fact that someone passing through this sleepy town not only loved his tree, but recognized *Christmas Wrapping*.

"Then let me welcome you to the Hidden Springs Inn and Spa. I'm Henry, and that overly friendly kitty at your feet is Zortea. Want me to help bring your bags in now, or are you hungry? Wait, she doesn't like..."

The words died in his throat as Zortea snuggled in the strange man's arms. The rather handsome strange man. She purred loud enough for Henry to hear over the music.

"Zortea, huh? Little Zee? I'm Steve, and you're about the sweetest magic cat I've ever met." He looked up at Henry.

"Just show me where the food is, Henry, and I'll help myself. I'm about half-starved."

Henry shook his head, trying not to stare at Steve.

At Zortea. He was trying not to stare at Zortea.

"That's one thing I can't do, leave you to fix your own Christmas Eve dinner. The owners would never forgive me. I honestly think they keep this place so they get to spoil new people rotten all the time. How about this? Come back to the kitchen and tell me what you want, and I'll get it started reheating. Then we'll get your bags."

Steve rubbed his nose against the strangely flirtatious feline's, laughing a wonderful huge laugh when she grabbed at his beard.

"She really *is* a magic cat. Sure, let's check out the food. I've only got one bag I'd need for the night, so no worries there."

Henry took Zortea, and his jaw dropped when she snuggled against his chest, too. What had gotten into Tingtanglia? He walked back toward the kitchen, hoping his hair wasn't a mess from leaning against the couch for so long.

The kitchen was as plain and industrial as the lobby was holiday fabulous. All stainless steel and stone and top-of-the-line appliances. The only nod to the time of year was a festive set of coffee mugs on the big prep table in the middle, decorated with vivid red poinsettias and candy canes. Henry set Zortea in front of her water bowl and opened the refrigerator that stood taller than he did.

"I'm not supposed to let people come back here, but since it's Christmas Eve and all, I'm hoping you won't report me."

"What a fantastic kitchen," Steve said, looking around. "I won't report you as long as you'll join me for dinner. I was supposed to be sitting down with my crazy family an hour ago, so I really would appreciate it."

Henry started to say he'd eat later, but at the sight of a bowl of mashed potatoes fluffier than the snow outside, his stomach gave out a grumble that just about echoed. After a virtuous and most heroic five seconds, both he and Steve burst out laughing.

"I guess I'd better say yes or my belly will start with the cuss words next."

CHAPTER 4

Steve took in a deep breath and let it out in a long, slow sigh. He'd never admit it to his mother as long as he lived, but that might have been the best Christmas dinner he'd ever eaten.

Rather than messing up the formal dining room for two people, he and Henry had carried as many plates as it took back out to that amazing lobby. Between the incredible decorations, the excellent food, and unexpectedly good company from both his host and the magic cat, Steve's holiday blues had lightened considerably.

Good as the food was—succulent ham and heavenly mashed potatoes and carrots spiced to perfection, just for a start—he'd kept focusing more on the conversation than the demands of his stomach. Now Henry knew about Steve's maddening but good problem of his cyber security work taking off much faster than he'd expected. Steve knew about Henry's excitement and fear of wrapping up his engineering studies and moving on to an apprenticeship.

Childhood stories, grownup disappointments with both of their big, close, and equally loving and infuriating families.

The good, the bad, and a little bit of the ugly when it came to dating. Thankfully Henry didn't fall into the complaining about how awful his exes were crap that got on Steve's last possible nerve. Sometimes things just didn't work out.

Finding out that their shared taste in music extended to movies and books, TV and travel. The biggest difference was Steve loved all the trappings and glamour of the holidays as much as Henry claimed to hate it. That twinkle in Henry's eyes when he talked about the decorations surrounding them was impossible to miss, though.

Steve hadn't talked nonstop for two hours to *anyone* for longer than he could remember. Not at work, not back home, and not with that breakup that was starting to feel quite a bit less painful.

A freakish Virginia Christmas Eve blizzard might turn out to be the best thing that had happened to him all year long.

Zortea, otherwise known the sweetest tabby cat in the world, cuddled in his lap again while they waited for Henry to bring out one final bit of dessert.

"I don't know about you, Tab-zanga," Steve said, "but I don't think I can eat another bite."

"Not even if it's fudge?"

Steve couldn't keep himself from grinning at the ceramic plate that looked just like a holiday wreath, piled up with pale brown squares. Henry sat beside him on the couch.

"That's not penuche, is it? I haven't seen that anywhere outside my parents' house for ages!"

"*That's* what it's called," Henry said with that low sort of giggle that was starting to make Steve weak at the knees. "Pen-nu-chi, you said?"

Zortea rearranged herself, chirping the whole time, until she was touching both Steve's leg and Henry's. She started kneading and purring up a storm of her own.

"Well, some of my dad's people up in Vermont say pen-noooch," Steve said. "I'm probably adding an East Tennessee twist. No matter what you call it, it's downright addictive."

He took a bite, humming deep in his throat. Smooth but crisp, with hints of caramel almost like a good praline.

"I didn't think I could eat another bite," Henry said, closing his eyes as he chewed. "But this is heavenly. I'm glad we had at least one thing you were looking forward to tonight."

Steve decided to listen when his heart said jump, at least to getting a bit flirty. His heart hadn't been paying much attention for the final few months of his last relationship.

Having it speak up again felt pretty damn good.

"Oh, I don't know, Henry. Much as I love traditional Tennessee holidays back home, surprises can be awfully nice, too."

Steve was relieved, and more than a little excited, to see Henry's slow smile and a shy, sexy flush on his cheeks. His full belly managed to move enough to turn warm little loops inside.

"I have to admit I wasn't expecting company at all tonight," Henry said, raising one of his eyebrows. "I'm glad my plans got changed, too."

Steve shifted, trying to move a little closer without being painfully obvious.

"You know, of all the decorations around this place, the one thing I haven't spotted is mistletoe. Seems like a strange omission if you ask me."

Zortea chose that exact moment to jump down and land on the rug with a resounding thump. She looked at Steve, then at Henry, her eyes glowing green from all the Christmas lights.

Then the magic cat trotted out of the lobby with her crooked tail flipped over her back, chattering and meowing to herself the whole way. Not toward the kitchen this time, but through another doorway off to the side.

"Did we just get scolded by a cat?" Steve said, trying his best not to laugh again.

"That wasn't a scolding." Henry's cheeks flushed even redder, but he was smiling as he glanced toward the doorway. "That was her making a suggestion. She does that a lot. She just ran toward the hot spring spa."

He turned to Steve then, with a half smile that sent the loops in his stomach up toward his chest, and further down. "That's where the mistletoe is, by the way."

"How about you show me that mistletoe?" Steve said. "And maybe join me in the spa?"

Henry leaned a tiny bit closer and shook his head, eyes half closed.

"I really should keep the lobby open. Just in case another lost traveler wanders in."

A buzz in his pocket and against his wrist pulled Steve's gaze away for a second, but after the first few words of the message he was glad of the interruption.

"My mom says they've closed the interstate, more than a foot of snow with more on the way. She's glad I stopped, hopes I can bring my new friend along for dinner when it clears up so they can say thank you for giving me such a warm and cheerful place to stay."

Zortea reappeared in the doorway, flipping her irregular tail back and forth. She let out a high-pitched meow that deepened into a growl that wasn't exactly threatening. Then she ran back the way she'd come.

"I don't care if it *is* a ghost," Henry said, barely loud enough for Steve to hear, before he spoke louder. "Sounds like it's time to close up for the night, then. I'm not about to ignore the magic cat of the inn. Now, about that mistletoe…"

ABOUT KARI

Cat-owned human Kari Kilgore's wanderlust and imagination lead her all over the world on grand adventures. Her heart and family (including the cats) bring her home to her native Appalachian Mountains of Virginia. From that solid base, she and her husband Jason A. Adams bring those adventures to life in fiction.

Kari writes fantasy, mystery, romance, science fiction, and contemporary fiction, and she's happiest when she surprises herself. She lives at the end of a long dirt road in the middle of the woods with Jason, various house critters, and wildlife they're better off not knowing more about.

The Confidential Adventure Club

For Kari's exclusive free After The End stories and deleted scenes, discounts, early pre-sale releases, adorable pet photos, and a whole lot more not available anywhere else, join us in The Club.

Hope to see you there!

www.KariKilgore.com
www.SpiralPublishing.net
www.ConfidentialAdventureClub.com

bookbub.com/authors/kari-kilgore

amazon.com/author/karikilgore

goodreads.com/karikilgore

facebook.com/kari.kilgore.1

ALSO BY KARI KILGORE

My furry muses and I hope you enjoyed reading the stories in *A Kaleidoscope of Cat Tales* as much as we enjoyed writing them.

You'll find more romance short stories, novellas, and novels at www.KariKilgore.com/Romance.

For more mystery and crime short stories, novellas, and novels, visit www.KariKilgore.com/Mystery.

If you love tales of fantasy, be sure to check out www.KariKilgore.com/Fantasy.

If you want more adventures from the Appalachian Mountains of Virginia and around the region, and in many genres, head over to www.KariKilgore.com/TalesFromAppalachia.

And of course, for more feline-forward yarns, visit www.karikilgore.com/Cats.

Be the first to know about release dates and check out more of my fiction, including almost every genre, at www.KariKilgore.com.

The Storms of Future Past Series:

Dreaming the Storm

Joining the Storm

Into the Storm

Fighting the Storm

Sensing the Storm: A Storms of Future Past Prequel

Storms of the Heart: A Storms of Future Past Romance

Storms of Future Past Books One through Four Collection

The Odd Society:

Independent by Means of Magic

Protected by Means of Magic

The Voices through Time Series:

Songs in the Mountain

Secrets in the Land

Walking the Ghosts: A Voices through Time Novella

Dispatches from the Galaxy Stories:

Restricted Species

The Becalmed

The Garbage Belt

Plurapod Pathogen

The Changes Cascade

Novels:

Until Death

The Dream Thief

Hand Me Downs

Protecting Her Own

Novellas:

Legacy of the Land

In the Pines

DNA Never Lies

The Box of Possibilities

Collections:

Fantastic Women: A Dark Fantasy Novella Trio

Fantastic Shorts: Volume 1

Near Future Forward (with Jason A. Adams)

Fantastic Shorts: Volume 2

Partners in Romance (with Jason A. Adams)

Dispatches from the Galaxy: A Space Opera Novella Trio

Fantastic Shorts: Volume 3

Escape into Romance: A Collection of Sweet Beginnings

Stepping Out of Reality: Short Spells of Appalachian Magic

Facing Down Extraordinary: A Series of Ordinary Heroes

Hacking Cybercrime: Dana Sanderson Short Mysteries

Shadows Mountain Deep (with Jason A. Adams)

Investigations Beyond Belief: The Initial Adventures of Deb Powers: Otherworldly PI

Passages in the Real World: Six Stories of Life's Transitions

Fantastic Side Trips: Side Characters Take Center Stage

ADDITIONAL COPYRIGHT INFORMATION